B[illegible] Bonds

Vampire Romance Short Stories

Kerry A. Campbell

Cover Design by Sherry D. Ramsey 2023

Campbell, Kerry A.

Email: funky_artist_22@hotmail.com

Web: https://thegeekybooklady.wordpress.com/

Cape Breton, Nova Scotia, Canada

Blood Bonds: Stories from the Lily and Quinn Series

Ebook ISBN: 978-1-9993829-0-2

Print ISBN: 978-1-9993829-3-3

"Awake and Alive" first appeared in *Undercurrents*, Third Person Press, 2008

"Airborne" first appeared in *Airborne*, Third Person Press, 2010

"Harvest" first appeared in *Unearthed*, Third Person Press, 2012

"Fever" first appeared in *Flashpoint*, Third Person Press, 2014

"Switch" first appeared in *The Good, The Bad, and The Funny*, Story Forge Writers Collective, 2018

Contents

Dedication

For Chris

My husband, my rock, my everything. Thank you. For everything.

My love for you is eternal. Until we meet again.

Awake and Alive

Lily pulled her coat closer against the crisp night air. Her cheeks stung, the skin tight from the cold.

Many people would feel uneasy walking alone after midnight down these streets. Lily did not. She knew her hometown well, and when her insomnia kept her awake, she hit the streets. After two years of these late-night walks, she felt comfortable walking alone.

But tonight Lily was not at ease. Something didn't feel right.

She stopped under the awning of an antique shop and assessed her surroundings. The street lights hummed with a life of their own. A stray black cat pawed through a dumpster nearby for morsels of discarded fish or meat. In the distance, a car engine whined on the deserted roads. Nothing out of the ordinary.

Lily continued to walk past the shops, nerves now jangling. Her cell phone was a comforting weight in her pocket. Unfortunately, her pepper spray was still at home, sitting on her bedroom dresser. She had never needed it before, but...she straightened and picked up her pace. Better get home.

Her apartment building was just ahead. As she hurried past an alleyway, the sound of a groan stopped her. She held her breath and waited, straining to listen. She took another step and heard a strangled cry of pain.

Somebody was hurt. She stood still, her legs feeling weak. She couldn't leave, couldn't turn her back on someone who needed help.

Lily peeked around the corner. The alley seemed empty, except for an open dumpster and battered boxes strewn around it. She was beginning to doubt what she'd heard, until something moved in the debris on the ground. It looked like a bloodied hand. The moan erupted again, more agonized. Someone was hurt badly.

Call 9-1-1 from here, she thought. She flicked her phone open. Damn. The battery was dead. Should she leave to call for help? Lily's concern kept her where she was. She had to check first.

Lily stepped into the alley.

"Are you okay?" she called out. "I heard you from the street. You sound pretty bad. My apartment is nearby. I'll run there and call an ambulance."

"No," a male voice growled.

No? The man was clearly in agony. His hand was slick with blood. She edged closer and nudged an empty box aside with her toe.

"Holy shit."

Thick chains wrapped around him. The stranger must have had just enough strength to pull his arm free. She found one end of the coil and frantically began unwrapping him. It wasn't easy. He was tall and the heavy chains encircled most of his body. As she worked, she was almost overcome by a nauseating stench. It took her a minute to realize that it was the smell of burning flesh. The chains had seared into the man's skin, though they were cool now to her touch.

She pushed the coil aside and knelt down beside the man. He held himself rigid, fighting the pain.

"I'm going to my apartment to call 9-1-1," Lily told him. "You need help. I promise to come right back." As Lily stood up, the stranger grabbed her wrist. He was incredibly strong for a man who looked like he had been hit by a truck.

"No, you can't do that," he said. His voice was deep and laced with pain. "I'll be fine now that those chains are gone."

Lily wondered if he was mentally ill as she surveyed his visible wounds. Fragments of his shirt hung in tatters. His bare torso was riddled with burns and his face was bruised and swollen. The blood she had seen earlier came from a slash across his bicep.

"Dude, you are seriously hurt. I can't just let you stay here like this. You need help."

"I'll be fine," he insisted.

"Typical male," she snapped. "You're a tough guy, huh? You can live with third-degree burns just fine, not to mention a few other injuries? Is pride getting in the way, or are you in some kind of trouble and the police are after you?" She looked down at him.

He stared back at her stubbornly. "You don't understand. Look." He released her wrist and pointed at his chest.

Lily watched in disbelief as the burns disappeared, leaving unmarked flesh behind. As she looked at his gash, it closed smoothly. Aside from the blood, there was soon only a tracery of white scars left as evidence of his injuries. Shocked, she studied his face again. The bruises and swollen lip had faded.

He was by far the most gorgeous man she'd ever laid eyes on.

"But...how...is that possible?" she finally managed to ask.

"I got the help I needed when you unraveled those silver chains. As you can see, I'm fine now. Thanks. I owe you. What's your name?"

"Lily," she said. She stood up, knees shaking beneath her, stunned by what she had seen. He rose and took her hand.

"Go home, Lily. It's too late for a young woman to be out. There are things that go bump in the night, you know. Take care." He turned, walked down the alley and vanished around the corner, leaving Lily dumbfounded.

Ten minutes later she crawled into bed. The encounter had left her confused and exhausted. She expected to lie awake, but she retreated into her blankets and fell asleep instantly.

After a rare good night's sleep, Lily woke to the sounds of the city. The autumn sun brightened her bedroom. The city hummed its everyday tune. Life was normal again.

She lay in bed, debating whether or not to get up. Staying up late took its toll on her, even if she had a good sleep afterward. She glanced at her clock. She had been asleep for seven hours, a rarity for her in the two years since her mother had died. Lily still couldn't seem to move on.

The memories came back in painful flashes. Her mother visiting. Lily in the kitchen fixing a snack, the sudden crash from her living room. Her mother on the floor, clutching her chest. Lily had held her mother tightly while she called an ambulance, but she was gone before help arrived.

Then, images from the night before rose. Lily curled deeper into the blankets. She could clearly see the man on the ground, covered in burns and blood. It sent shivers up her spine. And, even more unsettling, his skin healing and closing over so smoothly.

She caught a glimpse of her nightstand. Her current Stephen King novel sat on the edge. "Must have been a bad dream," she said aloud. "I was reading last night and when I fell asleep I had a nightmare. A damn vivid one, but just a nightmare." There. She felt better.

Tiny paws crossed her bedroom floor, and Duke jumped up beside her. The orange tabby cat had been in a dumpster when she found him last spring. He sported battle marks and an attitude, and she'd thought "Duke" was a tough enough name for him.

"Feeding time," she said as she got out of bed. She put on her blue fuzzy slippers and headed out to the kitchen, Duke following like a puppy.

She fed the fat tabby and frowned at the growing pile of take-out cartons on the counter. Lily hated her own cooking, but did she really eat out that much?

She began throwing the empty cartons into the trash and thought again of the sexy stranger. Too bad it had all been a crazy dream. She would love to see him again, and it had been months since she had been on a date. But it had been a dream; no real-life man could be as perfect. She sighed and bagged up the trash.

As crazy as she was feeling, sighing over imaginary men, she needed to see her best friend. She picked up her phone and dialed Stephanie's number. Lily had a standing date with Stephanie for Sunday breakfast at Joe's Diner.

"Hello?" a groggy voice said after several rings.

"Oh sorry, I didn't mean to wake you. You're usually up by now."

"That's okay, Lil. I was up late last night watching movies with Todd."

"Oh...I see. And is Todd still there?" Lily asked, teasing.

Stephanie sighed. "No, if he was I wouldn't have answered the phone. What's up?"

"Are we still on for this morning?" Lily could almost taste the diner's special brewed coffee. Caffeine would clear her head.

"Of course. I'll meet you down there in a half hour. Are you okay? You sound a little funny."

"Yeah, I'm fine. Just a rough night." An image of a bloodied body on the ground flashed before her. "See you soon!" She headed to her bedroom, threw on some clothes, and left the apartment.

The air was cool but crisp and refreshing. She took in a deep breath and closed her eyes. Peaceful everyday sounds surrounded her. Dogs barking, children playing in the park, and the odd car here and there. Sunday mornings weren't too busy. It was her favorite day of the week.

She realized she was following the same path as the night before. The alley from her nightmare was coming up. She almost stopped, but shook her head and continued on. "Stupid dream," she mumbled.

As she passed the alley, she glanced inside. Nothing there. Then again, what did she expect to see? It was like any other dirty alleyway. Dumpster, stray cats, garbage, a gleaming pile of metal...

Her breath caught in her throat. Beside the dumpster, the sun glinted off something metallic. She inched closer for a better look. Silver chains. She picked up some of the coils, and could clearly see where traces of dried blood darkened the links. The chains slipped from her shaking hands and clattered to the ground, waking a homeless man farther down the alleyway.

"Sorry," she gasped. She practically ran back to the street. She needed to get to Joe's and get some solid food.

She walked to the diner in a daze and looked around for Stephanie. Not here yet. The early morning rush was over, and Lily slid into a booth. The lingering smell of bacon made her stomach growl.

A moment later Susie, the waitress, walked over. "Girl, you look like hell."

"Gee, thanks, Susie."

"Sorry, I'm just saying. You see a ghost or something?"

Lily hugged herself. "Something like that." She took another deep breath, trying to calm herself. I'm not going crazy.

Stephanie arrived and Lily was glad of the distraction of ordering breakfast.

"You look horrible, Lily. Didn't sleep well last night?"

Susie poured them coffee before heading to another table. Lily drank some of the hot brew before answering. She felt like crying.

"I had this horrible dream—at least I thought it was—and then this morning—well, I found out it couldn't have been a dream," Lily rambled.

"Wait, wait, explain from the start," Stephanie ordered.

Lily began with the insomnia the night before and her late-night walk. Then, quietly, she told Stephanie everything that happened at the end of the walk. "I thought it was just a vivid dream until just a little while ago."

Stephanie stared at her for a long moment, frowning. Then she shook her head. "Well, of course it was just a nightmare. Nothing like that could actually happen."

"You don't get it, Stephanie," she snapped. "It wasn't a dream."

"What do you mean?"

Their breakfast came and they fell silent while Susie deposited plates. Lily found she'd lost her appetite. Pictures of the battered man and the blood-stained chains kept surfacing.

Once Susie left, Stephanie raised her eyebrows at Lily.

She sighed. "On my way here I found the damn chains in the alley, and they were coated with dried blood. And that was in broad daylight, after I slept like a baby for seven hours. Explain that. No way was that a figment of my imagination."

Stephanie sat in silence, chewing on her toast.

Don't tell me I'm a lunatic, Lily pleaded silently.

Finally, Stephanie met her eyes. "I don't know, Lily, I just don't know." She looked down at her plate and toyed with her food. "Something weird is going on, and I just want you to be careful."

Lily stared out the window. If it hadn't been a dream, what the hell was it? And where was the mysterious stranger now?

Quinn Carter opened his eyes to the comforting darkness. He stretched his limbs to work out the kinks. This wasn't the most comfortable lair he'd ever had, but the knots were a small price to pay. It kept him safe, from humans and the sun.

He emerged from the hole in the floor of the abandoned building, a single street light outside a dirty window providing the bit of light he needed. He surveyed his naked torso and arms. He had continued to heal during the day, and now not a trace of the burn marks or scars remained. He shuddered. The touch of the silver had been...horrible.

He dressed quickly. Time to hit the streets. He had work to do, starting with his heroine from the night before. He wanted to know who she was, and more importantly, if she had gone to the authorities. He had practically told her his secret. Hell, he had healed in front of her. She must have been freaked out.

Besides, it gave him a reason to see her again. There was something about her...an elusive something. She was beautiful, but it was more than that. He ignited when she touched him. Then again, he thought with a wry grin, if she hadn't, he would have quite literally caught on fire.

Quinn left the building through a door in the back, easily vaulted over an old chain link fence and strode through a thicket of trees. The crisp autumn air tingled on his skin. The moon was full and the sky was clear, millions of stars twinkling in the night. It was a good night to be alive. Or, in his case, undead.

He crept down an alleyway that led into town. Once he was on the darkened street, he relaxed. He couldn't risk his hiding place being found.

It was Sunday evening, so the streets were quiet. The few pedestrians were bundled in warm sweaters or jackets, hurrying to their destinations. In the shadows, a drug addict and a dealer held a swift conversation. Quinn liked having a lair near places like this. He fed from the people society swept under the rug.

He stayed alert and sniffed the air as he walked. Last night had been embarrassing. It was the first time anyone or anything had gotten the best of him. He clenched a fist reflexively. It was even more embarrassing that it was Creighton who had bested him.

Creighton had a reputation in the vampire world. There had been other slayers, but not many lasted long. Creighton was an old dog, hunting for twenty years now; he'd been on Quinn's scent for the last five. Last night he'd managed to corner Quinn in the alley, taking him by surprise with the silver chains. Creighton's face had twisted with pure hatred as he'd beaten the vampire.

Since Creighton had found him, Quinn had only one option. He had to go to Dimitri, his long-time friend and the head vamp for their region, and ask for help. The slayer wouldn't quit when he'd come so close.

Quinn knew where to look for Dimitri. As he walked briskly down the street, something caught his eye. Actually, it was someone. There she was, just up ahead. The woman who had saved his life. Lily.

Lily had decided to go for a walk a little earlier than usual. She had tried staying home, but once the sun went down and her apartment grew dark, anxiety flooded her. The memories of her mother's death would not leave her alone.

I'll be home before it gets too late. She was still freaked out about the night before. The memory of the encounter hadn't left her mind all day. She still had no answers.

She was almost home again when she caught sight of him. The man from her "dream" was heading her way. She glanced around. The streets were empty now. Okay, I knew it wasn't a dream! Her heart pounded in her chest. She didn't think he would hurt her, because he could have done that the night before. But her fingers still instinctively tightened around the can of pepper spray in her jeans pocket.

Even though nerves made her belly squirm, she couldn't help running her eyes over him. He was tall, over six feet, towering over her in a leather jacket, black jeans and cowboy boots. Shaggy, light brown hair, no longer matted with blood and dirt, fell over one eye. There was no sign of last night's trauma.

She couldn't move; she could barely breathe. She wanted to dash into her apartment, but her body was frozen in place, immobilized by an invisible force.

"Hello, Lily. I didn't think I'd see you again so soon. How are you?"

She stood staring for what was only seconds, but felt like an hour. Was he real?

"I...I'm fine," she stuttered.

"Don't worry, I won't hurt you." He smiled a grin that would make any woman want to fall into his arms. "I owe you one. I'm sure you have lots of questions about last night."

He seemed so confident, staring down at her with his warm brown eyes. Lily felt a hot flash of anger. All the fear and paranoia boiled to the surface.

"Yeah, you could say that," she snapped. "What the hell was that, anyway? I woke up this morning and convinced myself it had all been a bad dream! And now here you are, larger than life. You scared the crap out of me." Lily's eyes welled with tears, but she couldn't stop. "I thought you were a dead man, and the next thing I know, your wounds are healing and everything's just fine. And by the way, you don't owe me anything. I would have done it for anybody else." She was panting now, tears rolling down her face.

His face softened. "I'm sorry. I really am. Last night...last night I made a mistake that nearly cost me my life. And yes, I'm in your debt."

"Maybe an explanation, then?"

"You'd never believe me."

"Try me," she said.

He paused as if trying to decide what to say. After a moment he put his hand out to her.

"Take my hand," he said. "I won't hurt you. Please, trust me." Lily hesitated, thinking that she should just run inside. But she needed to know the truth. Cautiously, she lifted her hand and placed it in his. It was cold as ice. He moved closer and put his other hand on her forehead. She felt a sudden shock, like a jolt of electricity. It lasted only a few seconds and then Quinn released her.

"What did you do to me?" she demanded, shaken. She let go of his hand and pulled her coat in closer, hugging herself.

"I have...special abilities. I needed to find out what kind of person you are. I can trust you," he said. "I'll tell you what you want to know. The reason I healed so fast is that I'm a vampire."

Before she could react, a male voice interrupted them.

"Quinn, there you are."

So, the stranger had a name. Quinn.

"Dimitri. I was looking for you."

Dimitri looked over at Lily and back to Quinn.

"Oh, I'm sure you were," he said with a smirk.

"I was. I just had something to take care of first," Quinn said and glanced at Lily. "Just give me a few minutes."

Dimitri smiled. "I'll be over this way," he said and walked off into the shadows.

"I'm sorry," she began. "I don't sleep too well and it must be affecting my hearing because I would have sworn I heard you say 'vampire'."

"No, you heard right. I'm putting my life at risk telling you this, but when I looked into your mind I discovered that I can trust you. You're a rare human, Lily." He grinned. "And now you have your explanation."

He started to walk away, but she didn't want him to go. Not yet.

"Wait!" she cried. He turned around to look at her. All she could manage was, "Will I ever see you again?"

He smiled and said, "I hope so" before disappearing into the shadows, leaving Lily alone again.

"Creighton is near," Dimitri told Quinn after they sat down at a corner booth in a local bar.

"I know. He attacked me last night. I would have been dead if Lily hadn't come along." Quinn filled him in on the night before.

Dimitri gave his old friend a sly grin. "I can't believe that a girl rescued the big bad Quinn." He laughed.

"By the time she got there, Creighton had gone and I was writhing in an alley, literally frying." Quinn stared down at clenched fists, remembering. "If he hadn't had those chains, I would have killed him." Quinn remembered the look of panic on Creighton's face when the police cars drove by. He'd run then, leaving Quinn to suffer in the alley.

Dimitri's laugh faded and a grim look replaced it. "Nobody ever said that Creighton would play fair. You have the right to a piece of him, but I want to make him suffer and pay for what he did to my beloved. Understand?"

Quinn nodded. "Of course."

He knew Dimitri's history. Creighton had murdered Dimitri's wife and he wanted revenge. The one time Dimitri had his chance, the two had beaten each other to a pulp. Just before Dimitri went to make the killing strike, Creighton blew silver powder in Dimitri's face, allowing himself the opportunity to escape. Creighton had been too weakened himself to kill Dimitri.

"Good. I hear he's been hiding in an abandoned motel outside the city. I say we hit him tonight before he has the chance to come after one of us again."

Lily fretted restlessly in her bed. She fluffed her pillows and straightened her bedsheets before closing her eyes again and trying to settle down.

Tonight it was more than her insomnia at work. She couldn't get Quinn off her mind. It wasn't just him, it was what he had told her. If it was true, it could explain how quickly he had healed. But vampires were fiction, just creatures from books and movies, weren't they?

She opened her eyes and looked at her digital clock, the red numbers glowing *1:46*. Great. She couldn't stay in bed any longer, and she didn't think she could make herself go outside for a walk. Instead, she got up and went into her small living room and picked up a book.

Just as she sat down on her plush leather sofa, a knock sounded at her door.

This late? She reached under the sofa for the baseball bat she kept handy, just in case.

"Who is it?" She held her bat at the ready and stood just inches from the door frame.

"Officer Morris, Miss. I just have a few questions for you about a crime that took place outside a short while ago. I need to question any possible witnesses."

Lily looked out the peephole. A middle-aged man in a police officer's uniform was smiling into her line of vision.

"I know this is a hassle, but it won't take long." He took out a badge and held it up for her to see. Lily opened the door cautiously.

"Thank you, Miss. This will just take a minute." He took a notepad from his pocket.

"Did you see a young white man outside earlier? He's about six foot three inches, brown shaggy hair. Possibly wearing a leather jacket and cowboy boots."

Lily felt ill. Her gut had been right. She should have called the police after she helped Quinn. What had he done?

"Um...um, yes, I did. But only for a minute," she stammered.

He grinned, not pleasantly. It sent shivers up her body.

"Just as I thought," he snarled. "You're going to have to come with me."

Lily swung the baseball bat wildly. He grabbed it before it could make contact.

She turned and ran to her kitchen, yanking open the sink drawer in the dark. Just as she grabbed the cleaver, he was on her.

"Let me go!" she screamed. He held both her wrists with just one hand. His other arm held Lily against him.

"Now, now. Play nice, little lady." Lily tried to free herself from his grasp but he was too strong. "You'll pay," he said to her. "And so will they." He slid one hand up to her throat and squeezed. She gasped and struggled, but stars flashed in her vision and faded into blackness.

Lily had no idea how much time had passed when she opened her eyes. At first, her vision was blurry. Eventually her eyesight cleared, but it wasn't much of a help. She was in a shadowy mostly empty room.

Her hands and feet were bound, hands cuffed above her head to the wall, feet tied together with rope. The concrete floor was freezing under her bare feet. It reminded her of a movie she had once seen where prisoners were kept and tortured.

The door in the far corner opened and the phony cop walked in, no longer in uniform. He took off his black trench coat and put it on a table. Lily watched as he picked up a belt and fastened it on. The light caught something and she felt herself go rigid. A long knife hung from the belt. Objects clinked and clanged as he worked at the mysterious items. She didn't want to know what they were.

After what seemed an eternity, he flipped a light switch. A single dim bulb began to glow but didn't do much to illuminate the room. He turned and walked toward her.

"Don't come any closer!" she yelled.

He let out a howl of laughter.

"And what do you think you can do about it? I have you completely immobilized. Even if you weren't, you couldn't hurt me. You're just a pathetic female."

He shoved a dirty rag in her mouth, tying the cloth in a tight knot behind her head. She winced.

The friendly "officer" who had knocked on her door had disappeared entirely. His eyes now danced with evil in the dim light.

He unsheathed the long knife and fingered the blade. Lily tried to scream, but it was muffled by the gag.

"Oh, shut up. I'm not going to kill you." He started to pace in front of her, fingering the blade of the knife. "However, your vampire friends, those heathens, will." He lifted the knife and came closer to her. "You will be the perfect bait. They have your scent now, and when they know you're here, they will come to your rescue. But when they catch the scent of your blood, that will all change."

He reached out with the knife and delicately sliced the skin around her throat and shoulders. Lily screamed again as the blade pierced her flesh, leaving long wounds. Tears ran down her face from the excruciating pain. Creighton smiled. He cut her exposed arms, too, running the blade down the length of her forearm. "And one more for good measure," he said, slicing the blade across her stomach. He did it easily, as if she were a piece of meat, not a person. Lily kept screaming, the pain unbearable, but the gag stifled her cries.

"I don't know what Quinn told you, but it was all lies, I'm sure." He wiped the blade, almost lovingly. "When they smell your blood, when they see it dripping off you, they won't be able to stop themselves. And while they're busy with you, I'm going to kill them." He moved aside and Lily saw a gun on each hip. The knife slid back in place, beside one of the guns.

He took out one of his revolvers and opened the chamber to show her. It was fully loaded.

"Silver. One clean shot through the heart. It's the only way to kill 'em. I used to do it with stakes, but that's old school. Lot more fun this way. Less mess, too. And of course, there are the chains. It weakens them and burns their flesh. Almost thought I'd lost them. I had to pose as a homeless man during the day. It was the only way

I could get them back without being caught." He holstered the gun again and walked back towards the door.

The smell of her own blood thickened the air around Lily. It made her want to be sick, but she held back. Rivulets flowed hotly down her arms and neck and dripped down her chest.

"I won't be far away, darlin'. See, I can't be here when they arrive. They'll kill me if I am. I need them to start feeding on you first." And with that, he was gone.

"You sure this is it?" Quinn asked. He looked around the deserted building. It wasn't like any other place Creighton had hidden before.

"I'm positive. I had someone staking out the place. They've seen him here for the last few nights."

The two vampires approached slowly, hoping to take the slayer by surprise. Vampires were usually very quick, but there were times when it was a better advantage to take their time.

As they approached the basement entrance, Quinn caught a mingling of scents. Blood, for sure. But it didn't belong to Creighton. Creighton's scent was strong and vile. The smell of the blood was teasingly familiar, but Quinn couldn't place it.

They reached the side of the building and listened.

"Did you hear that?" Quinn asked.

Dimitri nodded. "Two hearts beating. One in the basement and one in the main level. But Creighton works alone. Who the hell is with him?"

Suddenly Quinn knew. He knew who the scent belonged to. It radiated off her in waves whenever he had been near her.

"Lily. He's got Lily. He must have seen her with me. He's using her as bait." Quinn felt a ball of anger and hatred explode inside him. His fangs slid out to their full length, glinting white in the moonlight.

Dimitri put a hand on his arm. "We'll get her. Now we know what he's up to. As long as he doesn't get the chance to use silver against us, we'll get him. And remember what I told you. I make the move that drains his life." Quinn nodded and his fangs retracted.

Dimitri tore the handle off the back door and they entered the dark building. The hallway was empty except for several old mattresses leaning against a wall. Once-elegant wall sconces lined the hallway and a threadbare carpet led into the rest of the building.

The heartbeat was close by, racing. It had to be Lily. The second heart beat fast as well, but not with the same urgency. It still radiated from the main level, but closer this time.

They moved down the hallway, all senses on the alert. Quinn sniffed the air when they reached another empty room.

"She's close by. Her scent is stronger here. There's blood, too." Quinn licked his lips. "Let's go that way." Quinn turned and passed an old supply room, and led them deeper into the building, Dimitri right behind him.

Quinn followed the scent to where it grew strongest, just outside the room in the corner. The door was open. Quinn looked in and saw Lily hanging up against a wall, blood running down her body in sluggish red streams.

Lily shivered with cold as her own hot blood poured down her body. She was growing weaker. The pain Creighton inflicted on her so casually made her nauseated. I can't die yet, she thought.

She had tried to wriggle free her hands and feet, but they were bound too tightly. In desperation, she had started to chew at the rag Creighton had used to gag her.

She thought she might be loosening it when a shadow caught her attention. The knot in her stomach tightened when she looked up and saw two figures standing just outside the door.

"You're going to be fine," one said in a low voice. She was sure it was Quinn, he sounded so calm and sure of himself. Surely he wouldn't really drink from her blood? She gnawed at the gag furiously, trying to free her mouth. She had to warn him about Creighton's trap.

They stood in the doorway, whispering, for what felt like hours. Why didn't Quinn free her? Her teeth and mouth ached from the gag, and she felt her resolve starting to break. They were blood-sucking vampires, after all. What were Quinn and Dimitri—she was sure it must be him—whispering about? She strained to hear them, but couldn't make out what they were saying. Finally, they entered the room where she was kept captive.

"Why has he done this to her, Dimitri?" Quinn shouted. "Why did he have to bring her into it? She's gagged and hung up like a rag doll. And..." Quinn trailed off.

"Creighton diced her and sliced her," said Dimitri. "Very clever. I never knew him to bait a vampire like that. He must be getting desperate."

They came closer, eyes fixed on her. To her horror, fangs extended from both their mouths as she watched. She tried again to scream and thrashed wildly. The gag loosened around her face, and she shook her head frantically. If she could speak, warn them, maybe Quinn would not kill her. After all, that would be twice she had saved his life.

Now they were mere inches from her face. Their bone-white fangs glistened in the light. She whimpered again when she saw their eyes fixed on the blood that dripped from her wounds.

"I'll bet her blood's not poisoned. It smells too sweet," said Dimitri.

Lily cringed as he leaned in and smelled her.

"I thought you liked her because she saved your sorry ass. I wonder if she tastes as good as she smells." He bent his head down and licked her neck. Lily sobbed helplessly. "Yeah, she does, Quinn. Have a taste. You know you want to."

As the vampires drew closer, Lily looked past them. Creighton stood in the doorway, revolvers pointed towards Quinn and Dimitri. Lily locked eyes with Quinn. She finally managed to spit out the rag and whispered, "He's behind you."

The two vampires spun around and seemed to vanish, reappearing next to the slayer. The two guns dropped to the floor with an echoing clatter. Quinn pinned Creighton's arms behind him. Dimitri plucked Creighton's blade from its sheath and buried it in the man's chest. Creighton gasped for air. Lily heard a snap and a blood-curdling scream as Quinn broke both Creighton's arms.

Quinn picked him up by his jacket collar and threw him against the wall. Creighton hit with a crunch and slid to the floor.

"You can have him," Quinn said to his friend. Dimitri smiled. He walked over to the crumpled form.

"I've been waiting a long time for this, Creighton." Dimitri dragged him out of the room.

Quinn went to Lily and pulled the rest of the tattered gag from her mouth and neck. "I'm getting you down from there." She could only nod in response. He quickly freed her from the cuffs and rope that bound her. Lily was so weak that her knees buckled and she slumped into his arms when she was finally free.

"It's going to be okay," Quinn crooned as he held Lily close. Her breath came in gasps against his chest. Quinn knew she had lost too much blood, but he didn't know how to help her.

Dimitri entered the room, his face a mask of gore.

"How is she?"

Quinn glanced down at Lily. Her eyes were closed and her body shook from shock. "She's lost a lot of blood."

Dimitri narrowed his eyes at his friend. "There's only one thing you can do. One way to save her."

Quinn looked at Dimitri. He understood immediately. But would she do it? Quinn picked Lily up and crossed the room to sit on a table. She stayed on his lap, her face hidden in his shirt like a scared child. "You'll be okay now," he whispered to her. She began sobbing hysterically. Quinn rubbed her back, trying to calm her.

"Lily, you're growing weaker with each minute. I can save you, but you have to let me." He cupped her face in his hand and looked at her. "Trust me."

He took out a pocket knife and rolled up a sleeve, then made a small slice on his exposed wrist. Blood dripped down his arm.

"Drink," he commanded.

Lily shook her head. "No! I can't!"

"You have to, Lily. It's the only way to help you."

"I don't want to be one of you."

"It doesn't work like that. This will make you stronger and help you heal. I don't want you to die here tonight. Drink my blood, and you will be fine. I promise it won't turn you." He stared at her intently, hoping she would accept his help.

Lily hesitated for another minute, hardly believing what he was asking her to do, but she had no options. She was too weak, her body felt like a dead weight. Slowly, she took his arm in her hands and began to drink. She gagged at first but forced the dead blood down her throat. Her stomach churned. Somehow she managed not to vomit. Eventually, Quinn pulled his arm from her and wiped her mouth clean with the hem of his shirt. His wrist was already closing.

"I'll take you home," he said.

"And I'll see you later," Dimitri said. "I think tonight calls for a celebration. Creighton is no longer a threat. I'll dispose of the body."

Quinn nodded to his friend. "Thanks."

Dimitri grinned. "Thank you. I'll be in touch. You know, I had planned for so long to draw out his torture. It didn't go exactly as planned, but it was good. Real good." His face sent shivers up Lily's spine.

"Th-thank you," Lily managed to say. Dimitri had been one of her rescuers, and she was grateful, but he scared the hell out of her.

"It was my pleasure," he said. Then, like a shadow, Dimitri was gone.

She looked at the slices on her arms. They were already beginning to heal. She shivered at the sight and tried to put it out of her mind.

Lily looked up at Quinn. "I thought you were going to kill me back there. Drink every last drop of my blood," she whispered. Her head rolled back and she closed her eyes. He brushed stray hair from her face.

"Never. Our plan was to kill Creighton tonight. We didn't think we'd find bait laid out for us. I'm sorry Creighton brought you into this." Quinn stopped.

Lily looked up at him and could tell he was upset.

"When we realized you were here, we knew Creighton was close by. We had to make it look good, or he'd have never come out of hiding. We wouldn't have hurt you. No matter how tempting you were." He smiled down at her. "We're not all murderous creatures like humans think."

"If I could move, I'd hit you right now. I thought I was a goner."

Quinn smiled. "Not as long as I can help it," he whispered. "Let's get you home. You've had more than enough for one night."

Lily woke, her head throbbing. She looked at her bedside clock. It was seven in the evening. The sun had dropped below the buildings and the street lights shone brightly. She had slept the day away. She had gotten up once or twice, but had been too tired to stay up.

It took her a minute to realize the heartbeat in her ears didn't belong to her. She looked at Duke, curled at the foot of her bed. She moved towards him, and the closer she got the louder the heartbeat became.

That is some messed-up shit! She couldn't bear the sound, so she left the cat in the bedroom and headed for her kitchen. She needed coffee—even her own awful coffee—and lots of it. By the time the coffee was brewed she felt calmer. Someone knocked on the door.

"Who's there?" she asked, although before the words were even out, she knew. She could sense him.

"It's me," Quinn said quietly.

She thought of telling him to go away and leave her alone, but she pushed that thought aside. After all, he did save her. She opened the door.

"Can I come in?" he asked.

She nodded, stepping back and holding the door wide. She couldn't help drinking him in with her eyes as he walked past her. He looked spectacular in his denim jeans and the black t-shirt that clung to his chest like a second skin.

"How are you feeling?" he asked. "You don't look as pale now. And your heartbeat seems fine."

"How do you know about my heartbeat?"

"It's something we vampires can sense."

"I didn't know that. Then again, up until a few days ago I didn't think vampires existed," she said, her voice sharp.

"There's a lot you don't know. The night holds many secrets."

"Then I don't want to know any more of them," she said. Well, maybe some of them, she thought as she looked at Quinn. Maybe there were a few things worth knowing. "I'm fine, by the way. Thanks. I just got up a few minutes ago."

She motioned him to follow her and they went into the living room. She sat in her recliner and he sat across from her on the sofa. Duke hissed at him and jumped into Lily's lap.

"I get that a lot," Quinn said.

"So. I drank your blood. I was able to hear Duke's heartbeat when I woke up. And I knew it was you at the door. What else is in store for me?"

He shrugged. "For a month or two you'll feel pretty good. You'll have more energy and you'll be stronger. But that will pass. What won't pass is that we'll have a connection to each other. If you're near I'll be able to feel your presence, your mood. And you will feel the same about me. That connection will last as long as you live."

"Oh, great! That's something I need in my life now, isn't it? I'll always be wondering if you're 'tuned in' to me," she growled. She looked over at Quinn and felt slightly guilty. He saved her life the only way he knew how. And maybe the idea was a little bit exciting. Just a little bit.

She smiled. "I'm sorry. I guess it could be worse. After all, you could have turned me into a vampire."

Quinn chuckled. "I think Dimitri would have liked that. I have it on good authority he wouldn't have minded keeping you at his side for a century or two."

Lily shivered. "Well, I'm glad that didn't happen."

"I can see your arms and neck have healed. Those scars will be gone in a day or two."

Lily looked down at herself. Thin pink lines etched her skin where the blade had cut into her. The pain the knife had caused left shortly after drinking Quinn's blood.

Quinn stood up. "I just wanted to check on you, see how you were. I'd better go."

Lily stood up and followed him to the door. "Wait!"

From the moment she had first met him, she had wanted to get to know him. Heck, she thought, I might even come to terms with the fact that he's technically dead.

Before she knew what she was doing, Lily stood on her tip-toes and kissed Quinn softly on the lips. "I never properly thanked you for saving my life," she said.

Quinn smiled. "That's the best thanks I've ever gotten." He tucked a stray hair behind her ear.

"Am I ever going to see you again?" she asked. She could feel something warm radiating from him. It was...happiness. Maybe this connection we have won't be too bad after all.

"You can bet your life on it." He turned and walked out the door. Lily ran to the window and looked outside. Quinn was nowhere to be seen. She tried using their bond to sense him, but he was gone.

"Drop by anytime," she said into the darkness. "I stay awake most nights."

Airborne

"Quinn! Isn't this the best party?" Dimitri raised his head up off the neck he'd been feeding from, blood dripping from his crimson lips.

"Yeah man, this is the best Blood Day ever," Quinn replied.

Blood Day. A holiday celebrated once a year by vampires all over the world.

Dimitri, oblivious to Quinn's lack of enthusiasm, said, "This year we've got more to celebrate!"

Vampires around them lifted their heads to the sky to scream their delight. "Rot, Creighton, rot!" they yelled.

News of the infamous vampire slayer's death, just weeks before, had spread quickly through the vampire community. They celebrated another year of survival, remembered fallen comrades, and rejoiced in the death of an enemy.

The tangy, sweet smell of blood wafted around Quinn. His nostrils flared, and his mouth watered, as the scent passed through his nose. It was intoxicating.

"Hungry?" Dimitri asked.

Quinn shook his head. "I'm fine," he said. Prior to the party, Quinn had fed briefly to temper his hunger. He didn't judge the others for taking lives, but he wouldn't do it himself.

"Hey Blake, why don't you finish him?" Dimitri asked. A sullen look crossed Blake's face.

"No thanks," he replied.

"Come on! I can share," said Dimitri. They looked down at the limp form of the man on the ground.

"Yeah, okay." Blake knelt on the ground beside Dimitri, and Quinn watched as Blake sank his fangs into the soft pink flesh. Quinn closed his eyes, remembering what it had been like to drain a human.

"No need to starve yourself. How come you didn't feed long ago?" Dimitri asked. Blake ignored him. Dimitri shook his head and let the vampire finish off the remaining blood.

Music filled the night air and Quinn surveyed the party. In the middle of an old farming field, vamps were enjoying themselves. In the center of the chaos, a bonfire crackled and danced in the darkness, shedding light on those who partied around it. The almost translucent skin of the vampires seemed to glow, their fangs glinting in the moonlight.

The aromas threatened to overwhelm Quinn. The musky scent of blood overshadowed the smoky smell of the burning fire. The fragrance of sex intermingled in the air. Everywhere Quinn looked, there were couples naked on the ground, grinding against each other.

"You know," Dimitri began, "that one over there has been eying you for a while. The night is still young, my friend. Why don't you take advantage? She's more than willing."

Quinn looked at the woman Dimitri spoke of. Blond and half-naked, she was motioning for Quinn to join her.

Quinn shrugged. "No thanks. Not exactly my type."

Dimitri turned to Blake who had joined them after feeding. "Can you believe this guy?" Dimitri's head shook, his black curls swaying with the movement. "That smoking hot chick wants Quinn and he's saying that she's not his type."

"Well, she is a bit of a skank, don't you think?" Blake asked.

Dimitri rolled his eyes. "I know why you're not interested in that," Dimitri said to Quinn, with a smirk.

"Oh yeah, and why would that be?" Quinn asked.

"Lily," Dimitri said.

"Isn't that the human who saved your life last month?" Blake asked.

Dimitri let out a whoop of laughter. It was a story he loved to tell to anyone who would listen.

"Yes," Quinn said, through gritted teeth. Everyone believed he was embarrassed that a female, a human one at that, had saved his life. But they were wrong. The embarrassing part for Quinn was that he had let Creighton get the best of him, getting himself lassoed with deadly silver chains.

"Lighten up, old friend."

Quinn glared at Dimitri. They had been friends for centuries and had been through a lot together. But every so often, Quinn felt the urge to deck him.

"I'm gonna go check out the action over there," Blake said, nodding towards the fire.

Quinn watched as Blake walked away. "Why would he let himself get that hungry?"

"Maybe your guilty conscience is contagious. I better not get too close," Dimitri said, snickering.

Quinn looked at his friend. He wished Dimitri would feel something for humans other than hunger, but Dimitri had avoided meaningful contact with humans for as long as Quinn had known him.

Best not to get friendly with your entrée. Spoils the flavor, Dimitri often said.

"So, have you seen her lately?" Dimitri asked.

"Lily? Yeah, I was with her the other night," he replied. "She's still uneasy, but she's coming around. I think Lily's still mentally digesting that we exist." Truth be told, he had been visiting her several nights a week. At first, she was reluctant to let him into her apartment. But now she seemed glad to see him.

"Think she'll be a threat to us?" Dimitri asked.

"No, not at all."

They walked through the throng of vampires, their agile legs deftly avoiding the party-goers.

"Dimitri!"

"Marcus, enjoying the party, I trust?" Dimitri asked. Marcus, a seven-foot-tall former football player, was Dimitri's right-hand man.

"Until a few minutes ago. I was over by the tree line with my woman when I caught a scent I didn't like. Hunter, for sure. Smelled like Jackson Black, the bastard who chased me in Alberta. Scent is pretty fresh," Marcus told them.

"I can see the turn-on for a hunter to want to crash one of these parties, but with this many of us, it's suicide," Dimitri said.

"What do you want to do about it? Search party?" Marcus asked.

"No, everyone is having a great time. Let's not spoil the night," Dimitri said.

Quinn looked around. A mad frenzy would ensue if word of a possible threat got out.

"I'll go with Marcus," Dimitri said. "Quinn, you go west and meet us at the other end of the clearing. If there really is someone out there, we'll catch him and bring him back. It'll be a nice party favor for our guests."

Quinn headed off through the throng of feeding vampires towards the tree line. A warm breeze rose. It stirred the branches, leaves falling to the ground.

"Wanna party, sexy?" a tall, brunette vamp asked, cutting in front of Quinn's path. Her fangs were extended, blood staining her chin.

"No babe, but I bet that guy does," he replied, as he pointed to a vamp clearly enjoying the attention of two other females. She smiled and went to join them.

Had it not been for meeting Lily, he might have taken the vamp up on her offer.

Since she saved my sorry ass, I can't stop thinking about her. He remembered clearly the night Creighton chased him down and bound him. Had Lily not come along and unraveled the chains from his burning flesh, he would have died in that alleyway.

Quinn reached the woods. After checking to make sure he wasn't being watched, he entered and began to sniff the air. The pungent aroma of blood wasn't as strong here. Quinn felt his muscles relax. It was hard being on a strict diet at a vampire bash.

He cast around, trying to catch a human scent. Not many people ventured this way, so he didn't think it would be too hard to pick up a trace of an intruder.

He walked, zig-zagging along the way, keeping his impeccable senses on alert. The only shadows in the trees came from a family of foxes, out on a hunting mission of their own.

Eventually, Quinn met up with Dimitri.

"Anything?" Quinn asked.

"We found the scent but lost it at the river. A hunter was definitely here tonight, but he's long gone now," Dimitri replied. "I told Marcus to go back to the party. I suggest we do the same."

Quinn and Dimitri headed back. Everyone continued to dance and play, blissfully unaware of the possible danger that had now passed.

"How you holding up, anyway?" Dimitri asked.

"I'm fine. Why?"

"Because every time we pass by someone feasting, your body goes stiff and your jaws clench. You could make an exception to your 'rule' once a year, you know," Dimitri said.

"I fed before coming tonight," he reminded Dimitri. While being around this much blood was testing his restraint, he was determined not to give in so easily.

A blood-curdling scream split through the darkness. The music abruptly ended and every vampire stopped. All heads turned to the source of the sound.

Quinn's sharp eyes scanned the area quickly. There by the fire, a female named Ginger stood, her arms wrapped around herself.

"It burns!" she cried, clutching her stomach. She began to cough violently, blood spurting from her mouth. She doubled over and collapsed on the ground.

The crowd around her watched in horror as her skin began to glow red, sores breaking out over her pale body.

She screamed in pain.

"Help me! Someone, please help me! It burns!" She writhed in agony.

Quinn took a step forward, but Dimitri grabbed his arm.

"No, Quinn. Stay here," he commanded.

"We have to help her!" Quinn insisted. He watched as other vampires rushed towards the retching woman.

Some decided it was time to leave the party. "I'm getting the hell out of here," Quinn heard one say before taking flight.

"Quinn, what's happening?" Dimitri asked.

Another vampire—a male this time—screamed in pain. Soon there were more, each one collapsing to the ground, blood spewing from their mouths.

"Let's get out of here, Quinn!" Dimitri said, fear thickening his voice.

Vampires took off in all directions, blending in with the shadows, rushing to fly off into the night, sprinting into the dense forest. Quinn watched as one female carried her partner's limp body away from the fury, tears streaking her pale face.

What the hell is going on here? I can't just leave my friends behind.

A tear welled and spilled down his own cheek as he watched. But I can't help if I succumb to this, too. Dimitri's right, we've got no choice but to leave.

He looked at Dimitri and nodded. With one final glance at the destruction behind them, they flew off into the darkness.

The dark-haired man pulled up his hood as he crept to the back of the brick building. The sound of laughter halted him in his tracks. Cool air whipped around him as he hid in the shadows. When all was silent again, he made his way to the door, unlocked it, and let himself in.

"Wow!" he exclaimed. He let out a throaty laugh. Adrenaline pumped through his body. How perfect tonight turned out! I knew the best way to test my creation was to expose it to a massive number of vampires. A smile crossed his face.

Nigel, his pet rat, sat in a cage nearby. The black rodent stared at him with small beady eyes.

The lab was becoming more and more dilapidated since he moved in three years ago. The white paint chipped, and he'd neglected to replace burned-out light bulbs. But he didn't care. He only cared about one thing.

"Just think, Nigel, if this goes well, I'll have my revenge. It will spread quickly through the air, affecting vampires everywhere." He ran his fingers through his short brown hair to stop the trembling in his hands.

He double-checked the locks to make sure they were secure before putting on his lab coat.

"I'll get them all, Nigel!" He dropped some food into the rat cage and watched as Nigel ate it greedily.

A warm sensation crept over him, making his skin tingle. His stomach knotted as panic set in.

"Damn, I thought I was careful," he said, running to the cabinet for a small brown bottle that sat inside.

The anti-viral. A nasal spray created in case of an emergency. He couldn't get his revenge if he was dead.

As his fingers curled around the small bottle, he took a deep breath to steady himself. The sheer comfort of having the cure at his fingertips made him feel better. The tingling stopped, and the knot uncurled itself.

False alarm...again! I'm turning into a hypochondriac, he thought, disgusted. The more he handled the virus, the more paranoid he became that he'd infect himself. At least, if there was exposure, he had the cure. He dreaded the thought of actually having to take it himself. The slow-acting anti-viral would work like a charm, but cause some pain in the healing process.

It had taken him a couple of years, but he did it. At least that's what it seemed like so far. A virus that would kill vampires. He had made sure to test the airborne virus on human blood before unleashing his wrath. He hoped his calculations would be right, that it would leave the human population unharmed.

He put the bottle safely back into the cabinet. Knowing it was in reaching distance eased his mind.

He walked to his desk and flipped open his laptop. He had been recording each part of the process. Now he had to document tonight's release of the virus. He typed for hours.

As the morning drew near, he grew tired. Getting up from his desk, he stretched and made his way to a storage closet, a musty smell hitting his nostrils as he opened the door. He lay down on the worn cot and closed his eyes. A smile crossed his face in his last moment of consciousness. *Finally, something has gone right for me.*

Things weren't looking good. For the first time since that night Creighton had chained him up, Quinn felt fear. His worry increased when he spotted Dimitri, and the grim look on his friend's face.

"Anything? How's Ginger?" Quinn asked. Luckily, the two of them were still well. But for how long? Quinn wondered.

"Dead," replied Dimitri.

"What happened last night?" Quinn asked, trying to steady himself.

"Apparently, several other vamps took her to their lair. She grew worse, vomiting when they fed her blood. Sores continued to break out all over her body." Dimitri paused, taking a breath to fend off a wave of tears that threatened to spill from his black eyes. It was the second time in his life that Quinn had ever seen this ruthless vampire appear vulnerable. Dimitri cleared his throat. "Ginger's friends watched over her. She died just before dawn."

"What about her friends?" Quinn asked.

"Two are dead. The other, Michael, has taken off. He delivered the message before leaving."

They walked down the street, taking care not to let anyone overhear them. They sat in the park gazebo, the planted flowers wilting with the approaching winter.

"Where's he going?" Quinn asked.

"He didn't say. He's so terrified to be around anyone that he left me a letter."

"Was it necessary for him to leave?" Quinn asked.

"I don't know. He told me in his letter that he thinks it's some sort of vamp flu," replied Dimitri.

"That doesn't make sense", Quinn said. "How could we come down with a flu?"

"I don't know, Quinn. He thinks a human virus is affecting us," Dimitri said.

"No, I don't think so." Quinn felt sure it was something more than that.

"Me neither, Quinn, but all we can do right now is guess."

"I haven't seen anything in the newspapers," Quinn said. "It looks as if the human race is safe from whatever this is. At least for now."

Earlier that night, Quinn had called a few friends. He found out that vampires all over the province had become ill, dying before the night was over. The numbers would increase if they didn't do something.

"What about Jackson Black? Marcus thought it was his scent he caught at the party. He could have had something to do with this," Quinn said.

"It's a possibility. We're going to have to figure out what hunters are in the area," Dimitri replied. "Quinn, there's something else."

"What?" he asked.

"If what we are dealing with here is something that affects vampires, it could also affect anyone with vampire blood," Dimitri said.

"Yeah, that makes sense," he replied.

Dimitri rolled his eyes. "Know of any humans with vamp blood running wild in their veins?"

"Lily," Quinn said. The knot that had formed inside his stomach tightened.

"You've got to go see her, Quinn. You need to warn her. If she does become ill, your blood isn't going to help her this time."

"You're right. Coming?" he asked, getting up to leave.

"She doesn't seem too fond of me, Quinn. I think I'll go see what else I can find out."

"Yeah, good idea. Hey Dimitri," Quinn called.

"Yeah?"

"Do you...do you have any idea what we're dealing with here?" he asked.

"No clue," he replied, and disappeared into the shadows.

"That's what I thought," whispered Quinn.

Lily pulled on her pale blue scrubs. Her job at the hospital suited her perfectly. Being a lab tech, she was able to work the night shift.

Getting kidnapped just weeks before by an insane vampire slayer hadn't helped her insomnia.

Lily's life had been ordinary before things recently took an interesting twist. That's what I get for wandering around after dark. But it's not like I could have left Quinn tied up to die, could I?

Later she learned Quinn was a genuine vampire. When she thought things couldn't get any crazier, she was kidnapped by the hunter and used for bait. Creighton strung her up and nearly gutted her like a fish. Quinn came to her rescue just in time. In order to save her life, Quinn made her drink some of his blood which healed her and gave her increased strength and hearing. That part had now worn off, but the other side effect, the bond she had with Quinn, would never go away until one of them died.

"And that's bound to be me," she huffed, angrily. Lily felt grateful that he had saved her, but she didn't want to be tied to a vampire for the rest of her life, though her thoughts on him had changed since their first encounter. She wasn't wary of him and even felt oddly relaxed when he came over. Lily was confused about her feelings for Quinn.

She was reaching for her lab coat when the doorbell rang.

The last time someone came to my door this late I got kidnapped.

She grabbed an old dented baseball bat that had been her father's and walked towards the door. As she neared it she began to relax, sensing who was there.

Lily opened the door and stared into the anxious face of Quinn. He smiled at her, but it wasn't his usual lop-sided grin.

"Hey," she said. "Where have you been?" She had a hard time reconciling the fact that she felt safer when Quinn was around because she knew she should be unnerved at being so close to a vampire.

"I've been…busy," he told her.

"Oh…well, come on in," she said, stepping aside. She watched as he shrugged out of his worn leather coat.

"So, how are you?" he asked, as he followed her into the living room.

"I'm fine. You okay?" she asked him, curious.

"Yeah, why?" he replied.

"Because you're fidgeting. I've never seen you do that before."

Quinn quickly crossed his arms to stop himself from further movement.

Lily giggled.

"What?" he asked.

"Nothing. It's just that I thought vampires were supposed to be all cool and collected. Guess not, huh?"

"I guess some of my human habits haven't gone away."

When she sat beside him on the plush burgundy sofa, butterflies in her stomach began a circus inside of her, flying and twirling everywhere. As much as she wanted to be afraid of him or deny what he was, she couldn't.

But that wasn't the only thing she felt radiating from him. Her bond with Quinn meant that she could feel his emotions. And right now she didn't like what she felt.

"Quinn, what's wrong?" The butterflies ceased their acrobatic moves.

Quinn stood, and she watched his tall frame pace the living room, his feet lightly touching the hardwood floor.

"There's a bit of a problem," he said.

"What?" she asked.

"Well, we don't know why but...vampires are getting sick and dying."

Lily let out a sigh. She had been afraid his announcement was going to affect her in some way. She did hope that Quinn wouldn't get sick. "Unfortunately Quinn, that's life."

He shook his head violently as he continued to pace. "No Lily, you don't understand. Vampires have lived and survived everything, including the Black Plague. There are very few ways in which we die, and illness is not of them," he said.

"I haven't heard of any outbreak on the news," Lily told him, concerned.

"This outbreak, whatever it is, won't be on the news. I've been talking to Dimitri."

At the mention of his name, Lily felt a chill run down her spine. Dimitri was downright scary. She pulled the throw off the back of the sofa and wrapped it around herself, bracing for whatever Quinn was going to tell her. "What does he think it is?"

"He's not sure, but whatever it is, it seems to only affect vampires. We can't figure it out. I witnessed what it can do, Lily." He sighed. "It's...horrible. Our body's way of healing...well, we aren't able to."

"Where do I fit into all this?" Lily asked. She knew she did. The worry she felt from him was directed at her. She sat on the edge of the sofa, clutching the throw tightly.

He sat beside her then, and took her hand into his.

"You have vampire blood in your veins." Quinn looked down, unable to meet her gaze. "It's a small amount, but you've got it."

Lily recoiled, pulling away her hand. "So you think there's a chance I could get whatever this is?"

He looked up at her, worry evident on his face. "You may not get it, but you're at risk."

She jumped up off the sofa, the blanket tumbling to the floor. "Ever since I met you there's been nothing but trouble." She chewed her bottom lip, forcing back her tears. Lily turned away as Quinn stood up to go. He paused, looking at her.

"As crazy as it sounds, I love you, Lily. I'm not going to let you die because of me."

When Lily turned around, Quinn was gone.

She debated calling in sick to work but thought better of it. She was too upset to stay at home. She grabbed her lab coat and left.

It was a typical Monday night at the hospital. The regular hypochondriacs sat in the emergency room while a few urgent cases were being tended to. Lily headed to the break room for a coffee before her shift started. She needed something to steady her nerves. Her head still reeled from the bomb Quinn dropped on her.

She poured herself a cup of the black sludge and sat down. She closed her eyes and let the hot liquid seep into her. Everything Quinn told her kept surfacing in her mind.

The door to the break room burst open, stirring Lily away from her thoughts.

"He thinks he's so important. God, I hate men like that. Oh, hey Lily."

"Hi Kendra. Who thinks they're so important?" Lily asked, not really caring, but trying to get her mind off Quinn's news.

"That Dr. Conrad, who has his lab down in the basement. He throws a fit if anybody goes down there, even the cleaning crew. He'll get away with it too, the pompous bastard."

"The hospital actually allows a lab in the basement?" Lily asked.

"Yeah, but it's only because he donates a huge amount of money to the hospital every year," Kendra said.

"I guess when you've got money, you can get your way," Lily commented.

"I wonder what he's researching. Probably inventing new ways to be an asshole," one nurse said as she reached for the coffee pot.

"I hear he's on the edge of a breakthrough. Something to do with creating a virus to eradicate cancer," Kendra said.

"Whatever he's doing down there, it doesn't give him the right to be an ignorant jerk."

Lily let her mind drift again as the nurses chatted away. As she sipped from her mug, an idea formed in the back of her mind. If it's a flu the vampires are up against, then it can't be anything natural. Is it possible someone created a virus, specifically to kill vampires? She knew of genetically engineered viruses, and their use in the war against cancer.

She got up from the table and headed off to start her shift.

His dark eyes shimmered with excitement. Everything was going according to plan. His first test was proving to be a success. He had been out trying to find out information, listening from the shadows. From what he overheard, many vampires were dead. Panic was building. And he had been right about one thing; the virus was spreading.

"Everything is going so well, Nigel. I think another test is in order." He looked over at the fat rat, who quietly nibbled on a piece of cheese.

He paced the floor, his mind racing with possibilities.

"But where should I try it next? The party was the best place...so many there." He chewed on a hangnail as he thought. The only sound was from Nigel eating. He leaned over the table, eyebrows furrowing in concentration. Finally, an idea came to him.

"I have to stay close by," he said, his voice even, "but I could go over into the next town. There's a large underground coven there. I'll head out tonight, take a vial, and let it loose in the park."

He stood, ripped off his lab coat, and went to his supply closet. He quickly changed into black jeans and a black hooded sweater. Then he went to his refrigerated storage unit and opened it up.

Bottles of his creation stood in neat rows. He ran his fingertips lovingly over the tops of them, pleased with his work. He planned to let them out locally at first, and in time globally, until every vampire was dead. He carefully removed a bottle and put it into his pants pocket. He smiled at the possibilities before closing the lid and locking it.

"Oh, I almost forgot!" He went to the cabinet containing his anti-viral. He put the small bottle in his pocket, just in case. He breathed easy knowing it was close at hand.

Soon, every bloodsucker will be dead, he thought, as he left to unleash another batch of his creation.

Two nights had passed since Quinn spoke to Lily. He knew she needed some space, and he would let her have it. When his cell phone rang, he was surprised to see Lily's name come up on the screen.

"Hello?"

"Hey, Quinn. Um, how are you?" she asked.

"I'm okay. How are you holding up?"

"Pretty good. Ah, listen, Quinn, you threw me for a loop the other night. I'm sorry for freaking out on you."

"It's okay, babe. I kinda expected it."

"Well, I really am sorry. Listen, I've been thinking a lot about what you told me the other night. I have an idea. It's not much, but it might be something to go on."

Quinn was definitely intrigued. He and Dimitri had been working hard trying to figure things out but kept coming up short.

"Any idea is a good idea at this point. What is it?"

"Well, I think that this could be man-made. Since your race has been able to survive horrific illnesses, it only makes sense that this isn't Mother Nature at work. At the lab, I've heard all sorts of discussions on man-made viruses. Doctors have started using genetically engineered viruses to fight cancer and other diseases. Maybe someone has created one to make you sick. Does this make any sense, Quinn?"

"It does. The problem is, I have no idea what hunters have that kind of knowledge. I'll have to talk to Dimitri about this. He may have some idea. Thanks, Lil, you just helped us out a lot."

"Well, it's the least I could do," she said. "Be careful, okay?"

"I'll be fine," he said, not knowing if that statement was true.

He said goodbye and then quickly dialed Dimitri's number. Quinn filled him in on Lily's theory.

"It's brilliant. This hunter must be some sort of evil genius. Think about it, Quinn. What better way to hunt vampires? Create a virus and let it spread, killing hundreds if not thousands. He gets to sit back and let it do his dirty work. What a sick, twisted son-of-a-bitch."

"But who the hell is making it?" Quinn asked.

There was a long pause before Dimitri spoke again.

"I'll be over there in a while. I've got a few calls to make," Dimitri said and hung up.

Quinn began to feel hunger grow inside of him. It was like a ball of fire in the pit of his stomach. He hadn't fed since the night of the party. If he didn't feed soon, he'd lose his self-control.

Quinn pulled on his beaten leather coat and headed outside. Down the street from him was a crack house. People were in and out of there constantly. He just needed to snag one wasted junkie, and he'd be fine.

He lurked in the shadows nearby, patiently waiting. Heat flared in his belly and he closed his eyes against the burning sensation.

It was fifteen long minutes later when Quinn heard the door creak open. Quinn watched with keen eyes as a young man stumbled out and down the street, heading in his direction. In just a few minutes, Quinn had lured him down a dark alleyway and fed from him. He left the addict propped up against the building. It was a mild night, and in a few hours he would wake, not remembering a thing. When Quinn got back to his lair, Dimitri was there waiting for him.

"What's that?" he asked, pointing to the paper Dimitri held in his hand.

"There are five hunters in the province, three of whom happen to be close by. I have their names and locations right here," Dimitri said, waving the piece of paper in front of Quinn.

Quinn snatched the paper from Dimitri, and read it out loud.

"Sam Parker, vampire hunter and former marine." Quinn looked up at Dimitri. "He sounds like the kind of man who would have good connections."

"Keep reading," Dimitri said.

"Hey, this is the guy Marcus mentioned at the party. Jackson Black, former microbiologist. Shit Dimitri, this could be our guy."

"Has good motive, too. Caught a newbie vamp feasting from his twin daughters. They were only five. By the time he got there, it was too late. He's been bent on revenge since."

Quinn laughed when he read the third name. "Molly Turner. I haven't heard her name crop up in a while."

"Yeah, she's been inactive lately. But she's in the area so we need to check her out. There's another thing I meant to tell you. You're not going to like it."

Quinn's eyes narrowed. "What?"

"We need Lily's help."

"No way in hell, Dimitri."

"We need her, Quinn. She's the only one we know who can get close enough without tipping them off. If they get one sniff that we're stalking around, we're going to have another problem on our hands."

Quinn sighed. He didn't like it, but Dimitri was right.

"I'll ask her, but I won't force her."

"Then I'll do what you won't."

Quinn hissed. "If you touch one hair—!"

"Relax, relax. If I know that fine creature like I think I do, she's not going to say no to you."

"Okay," Quinn huffed. He looked down at his watch. It was too late to do anything tonight. "She's at work but I'll leave a message."

"Very well."

Reluctantly, Quinn took out his cell and dialed Lily's number.

Lily yawned as she headed down the hall to the blood bank. She checked her watch. Once she took the bags down to the ER nurses, she'd be free to leave.

She reached the door and peered inside. She was appalled at what she witnessed: one of the doctors took several bags of blood, not bothering to sign them out on the clipboard. She ducked away from the window, hoping she hadn't been spotted. When the door swung open, he bumped right into her.

"Sorry," he said, curtly.

Lily wasn't one to stir things up, but she had to say something.

"Excuse me, doctor, I think you forgot to sign those out." Lily read his name tag. Dr. Conrad.

So this is the guy the nurses were bitching about.

"Who are you?" he asked, his voice gruff.

"Lily Myers, one of the night shift lab techs. I didn't mean to offend. It's easy to forget little things when you're busy."

"It's none of your concern. Don't you know who I am? I suggest you keep your nose out of my business." He turned on his heels and headed for the elevator.

What a pompous ass.

Lily took the bags down to the nurses' station, and ten minutes later she left the hospital. As she got into her car, she was still on edge from her encounter with Dr. Conrad. She flipped open her cell phone. An alert for a missed message flashed on her screen. She called her voicemail and listened.

"Hey Lily, it's Quinn. Ah, I told Dimitri your theory, and we've come up with a few suspects. Um...we kinda need your help. Just a little investigating, nothing serious. Okay, call me."

Lily groaned and hung up the phone. Just great. She called him back. After three rings, he answered.

"What did I do in a past life that made me deserve this?" she asked.

"I knew you wouldn't like this. Trust me, it wasn't my idea," Quinn told her.

"What is it that you need me to do?" she asked.

"We've got a few suspects. All you've got to do is get close enough to assess the situation."

"How come you can't do it?"

"Lily, these are seasoned hunters who know who we are. If I walk up to the door and knock, there'll be problems. We've got a plan. You'll be safe, I promise," he said.

Lily huffed. "Okay, I'm off for the next two nights. You and Dimitri can come over tomorrow evening."

"Thanks, this means a lot."

"Yeah, well, I want this problem solved, too."

"You feeling okay? You sound a little off," Quinn inquired.

"Yeah, I'm fine. I just had a run-in with one of the doctors. He thinks he can get away with anything because he donates a huge amount of money every year."

"Want me to take care of him for ya?" Quinn asked.

Lily giggled. "I certainly hope you're joking."

"That depends on if you want me to do it."

"Good night, Quinn!"

Lily sighed and shut her phone. As she drove the deserted streets home, she considered the possibility that the rest of her life might be intermingled with a vampire's.

Winter was Quinn's favorite time of year. The early sunset meant he was awake earlier. It was almost five o'clock when Quinn knocked on Lily's door, Dimitri at his side.

Quinn had immediately gotten in touch with Dimitri when Lily agreed to help.

"I wouldn't dare disappoint a beautiful creature like her," had been Dimitri's reply when he heard that Lily wanted them both to show up the next night. Quinn had to quickly stifle the jealous feeling that crept up on him. Something about Lily made him feel ...territorial.

I could never tell her that. She'd skin me.

They could hear the soft padding of her feet as she walked to the door.

"Hey, come on in," she said, her voice wavering. Quinn could feel her nervousness a mile away. Not only did she have to help vampires, but one of them happened to frighten her.

"Are you sure you're okay with having me inside?" Dimitri asked.

"Yeah, of course," she replied.

"Behave yourself," Quinn warned as they entered the apartment.

Lily's cat, Duke, hissed as they entered. Dimitri hissed back and laughed at the retreating tabby. Quinn glared at his friend. Dimitri shrugged an apology.

Quinn eyed Lily. She wore a dark blue hooded sweater and dark jeans. Her brown hair was tied back in a severe ponytail.

"You look like you're ready to rob a bank," Quinn said, laughing.

Lily scowled. "Well, I feel like it. I have no clue what's planned for me. I suppose this was your idea," she said, looking at Dimitri.

Dimitri scoffed. "I assure you, I don't like the idea of a human helping. However, we have no other choice."

Lily ignored the dig. "All right, what is it I'm getting into here anyway? I don't like the idea of confronting a bunch of slayers." She shivered. Quinn knew she was remembering her last run in with a vampire hunter.

"There's no need for you to worry. You're not going to be in any danger," Quinn promised.

"We'll be close by, but not close enough for them to sense us. If we hear any struggle on your end, we'll come to the rescue," Dimitri assured her.

"Okay, so how am I supposed to get information?" she asked.

"It's simple. What kind of person would visit a slayer?"

Lily thought for a moment. "Someone who wants a vampire dead."

"Exactly. You'll act as if you've had a close encounter with a vampire, and want them dead. Think you can do that?" Dimitri asked.

"That won't be hard to fake," Lily said as she looked at the two formidable vamps. "Let's do this."

Lily stood on the doorstep, trying not to shiver. A gust of winter wind whipped around her. She had her hood over her head, trying to keep warm. I should have worn a coat. She knocked on the door a second time.

"I'm coming, I'm coming," a woman called.

A short woman with tangled blond hair opened the door, a cigarette hanging from her mouth.

"What ya want?" she asked.

Lily turned to look behind her, making sure nobody was around. "Um, are you Molly Turner?"

The woman took her cigarette from her mouth and blew pungent smoke in Lily's direction. Lily held her breath, trying not to inhale. "Yeah, what of it?"

Lily steeled her nerves. You can do this.

"I need some help. I was told you'd be able to," she said.

"How the hell am I supposed to help you, doll face?"

"I need someone dead. A vampire."

Molly's eyes grew round as saucers.

"Get in here," she growled at Lily.

Lily did as she was told, and followed the woman inside. Molly sat at an old table and motioned for Lily to sit down with her. Lily watched as Molly took out a flask and downed a big swig.

"How did you know to come to me?" she asked, eying Lily suspiciously.

"I was attacked by a vampire a few weeks ago. When I told Creighton, he sent me to you," she lied. It was a big risk. She didn't know if the hunter community knew he was dead.

The woman shook her head. "That old coot. I'm surprised he didn't sign on for the job himself. Why didn't he? And how do you know him, anyway?"

Lily looked the woman straight in the eyes and leaned in closer.

"He used to be a friend of my uncle's. When I asked him for help, he said he was on the way to do a job on the other side of the country." Lily took a deep breath, not knowing if this woman believed her story or not.

"I guess that's why I haven't heard from him in a while," Molly said, lighting another smoke.

"So, would you be able to help me?" Lily asked.

Molly took a long drag from her cigarette.

"Sorry kid, can't."

"What? Why not?"

"I gave it up. I had to. My father...he's not well. So I came back here a year ago to take care of him. I'm the only one he's got." She looked at Lily, sadness in her eyes.

Lily left a few minutes later, meeting Quinn and Dimitri the next block down. Quinn was sitting behind the wheel. She could feel him relax as she neared.

"So, what happened?" Quinn asked.

"It's not her. She gave hunting up a year ago to take care of her sick father."

Quinn huffed.

"Calm down, old man," Dimitri said. "We knew the chance it was her was slim. That's one down, two to go. Let's hit the road."

Quinn started the car and drove across town.

"This isn't where I pictured a former marine would live. Are you sure the address is right?" Quinn asked as he eyed the run-down apartment complex.

"Um, did you just say 'former marine'?" Lily asked. Dealing with another woman was one thing, ex-military was another.

"Yes, Quinn, this is the place," Dimitri said. "And yes Lily, you heard right. Don't worry. You'll be fine."

"Why is he a suspect?" Lily asked.

"He'd have the right connections to have something like this virus created. It's number eight, the apartment on the end."

"You okay?" Quinn asked.

"Never better," she said sarcastically. Lily got out of the car and briskly walked to the apartment. A television blasted from inside.

She rang the doorbell and hoped for the best. She turned to look toward the car. It was gone.

The door creaked open. A bored-looking teenage boy answered.

"Hi, um, I'm looking for Sam Parker. Is he home?"

The boy rolled his eyes. "Dad! You got a visitor." Then he looked back at Lily. "He's in the den," he said, and pointed inside. He turned and ran upstairs, slamming his bedroom door shut.

"Who is it?" Sam bellowed.

Lily hesitantly walked inside. A well-built man in his forties sat in a wheelchair, intently watching an old war movie. He had a brush cut, and eyes that never left the screen.

"Hello?"

Her voice startled him. He looked quickly at her before turning the television off.

"Who might you be?" he asked, wheeling himself closer.

"I'm Lily. I was told you may be able to help me."

"Who sent you?"

She began to feel nervous. He looked as if he could take her and snap her in two. His arms were bursting with muscles.

"Creighton," she said.

"Need a vamp killed, huh?" he asked, staring her down.

"Ah, yes sir."

Sam Parker burst into laughter. "That old bastard knows I'm in a chair. I haven't hunted in almost two years. Had a run-in that left me sitting in this for the rest of my days," he said, and banged his hands on the wheels. "Why did he send you to me?"

Oh shit.

Lily's mind began to spin, quickly thinking of a good response.

"He's in the middle of another hunt. Said you might know someone that could help." When she was a kid, she could lie herself out of any sticky situation. Apparently, it was a skill she had never lost.

"Sorry, but I haven't kept in touch with any of 'em except for Creighton, and that hasn't been very often."

Lily feigned disappointment. "All right then. Thanks anyway," she said.

He went with her to the door. "Get in touch with the old man again. He'll probably take the job himself once he's done this one. Don't worry sweetheart, someone will kill that blood-sucking beast for you."

Lily inwardly winced as she nodded her thanks.

"So?" Quinn asked, once she was in the car.

"Not our guy. He's been in a wheelchair for a while," she said.

"Damn it," Quinn said. He turned to Dimitri. "I think you better find someone more reliable to locate hunters."

"Tell me about it. Anyway, you know what that means, Quinn. This Jackson Black has to be our guy," Dimitri said.

"And what do we do if it's not?" Quinn asked, clearly growing impatient.

Dimitri was silent, while Lily cowered in the back seat. She didn't care to see Quinn enraged.

Quinn shook his head and started the car. He began to drive the thirty miles it took to get to Jackson's cabin. On the way, Dimitri filled Lily in on why Black had become a hunter.

"That's horrible," she said. She didn't think it was right to be out killing vampires, but she understood the man's reasoning. To lose both children to a hungry vampire...she shivered.

"It's almost over," Quinn said gently, trying to comfort her.

"I know," she replied.

As they neared the cabin, Lily took in the surroundings. It looked like a set from a horror movie. An old log cabin lurking deep in the woods. The moon was full and bright, and somewhere in the distance, a wolf howled.

"Hey Quinn, check out that out," Dimitri said. Lily looked in the same direction, but it was too dark. She didn't have the eyesight they did.

"What? What is it?" she asked, panicked.

"The door. Look."

As the car drew nearer, the lights skimmed the front of the home. She could see what they had been looking at. The door to the cabin hung open by its hinges.

Quinn turned to look at Lily.

"Stay here," he told her, as Dimitri got out of the car.

"I'm coming too," she protested. Quinn had no time to argue.

Quinn and Dimitri made it to the cabin, Lily running behind.

"You're not going to want to come in here," he said.

"Like hell I'm not. You get me to—" Lily stopped dead in her tracks. Her face turned green in the moonlight.

"Oh, you were right," she said, then turned and threw up in the bushes.

Even though she was still outside, it was an assault on the senses. The stench was awful. A pungent, rotten odor drifted up their noses.

Quinn surveyed the room, hardly believing the sight that lay before him.

A man—what was left of him—lay in the middle of the floor. A pool of congealed blood surrounded him.

"He definitely knew something," Dimitri said, nonplussed at the sight. "I'm going to check out the rest of the place."

Quinn could still hear Lily retching outside of the cabin. He walked over to the body to get a closer look.

The buzzing of flies greeted Quinn as he knelt down to examine the body. The head had been ripped off, leaving tissue hanging from what was left of the neck. The skin was stained with blood. Most of his clothes were torn off except for a few shreds around his waist. Quinn looked closer at the flap of open skin on the chest. Maggots feasted on the flesh inside the chest cavity.

"Heart's been ripped out," Quinn said, not realizing Lily overheard him.

"Oh, you did not just say that," Lily groaned, beginning to heave again.

Quinn looked around the room for the head. It took a few minutes, but when he searched under the sofa, dead eyes stared back at him. A distended tongue lolled out of bluish-gray lips.

Quinn reached in and grabbed the matted hair.

"Find anything interesting?" Dimitri asked.

Quinn stood up and held the bloated head for Dimitri to see.

"Yeah, that's Jackson Black, all right," Dimitri confirmed. "I found his lab, or at least what's left of it. It was torn apart, but whatever research he'd been doing is gone. Someone knew what he was doing."

Quinn tossed the head down by the rotting corpse of Jackson Black. "So what are we going to do about this mess," Quinn asked, gesturing to the devastation that lay before them.

"Fire," Dimitri said.

While Dimitri rigged the old gas stove to explode, Quinn ran back to the car. Lily lay in the back seat, holding her stomach. Quinn leaned over to stroke her hair.

"You okay?" he asked.

"Yeah, I guess. I just wasn't prepared for...that." She gulped, holding back the nausea.

Dimitri opened the passenger side door and leaped into the car. "Let's beat it," he said.

Quinn started the car and peeled the car down the driveway, dirt flying in their wake. An explosion rang out, leaving the cabin engulfed with flames, burning the remains of Jackson Black.

Lily woke, her body sore. Her ribs and back ached from the heaving she had done. Quinn and Dimitri wouldn't tell her what else had been in the cabin, leaving Lily to believe that what she had smelled had just been the leading edge of the horror.

She slept most of the day, knowing she would be out with Quinn again. Three suspects had been crossed off the list, leaving someone unknown out there doing this horrible thing.

Lily stretched and crawled out of bed, making her way to the kitchen. Her stomach growled. She made toast and ate slowly, not wanting to overload her sensitive stomach.

She felt Quinn approaching and opened the door just as he was about to knock.

"Hey," he said, smiling.

"What are you smiling about?" she asked.

"You look cute with your hair tousled like that," he replied.

Lily lifted her hands to her head. "I just got up fifteen minutes ago. Let me get a quick shower."

"No problem," he said, and kissed her.

In the shower, Lily closed her eyes and let the hot water cascade down her sore body. Her muscles began to slowly unkink. She didn't know what she was in for tonight, so she gladly took an extra few minutes to relax.

She emerged a half hour later, wearing a blue coat and jeans.

"Where are we going tonight?" she asked, as they headed down the street.

"To see Dimitri. You holding up okay?"

Lily shoved her hands deep into the pockets of her coat. "It's just weird. Hanging out with vampires, investigating slayers. But, yeah, I'm doing okay. Last night I was scared, but knowing you were nearby made me feel safer."

Quinn put his arm around her and pulled her close. "As long as I'm around, you'll always be safe."

They were nearing Dimitri's lair when Quinn halted in his tracks.

"Hey Blake! Blake!" Quinn cried out.

Lily looked up. A tall, broad man was walking towards them.

"Hey Quinn," a deep voice said.

When his face came into view, Lily almost collapsed. Had it not been for Quinn holding onto her, she probably would have.

"Lily, this is Blake," Quinn said. "A friend of mine."

"Hello, Dr. Conrad," Lily said, her tone cool.

"How do you two know each other?" Quinn asked, confused.

"We work at the same hospital," Blake said. "I didn't realize though, that this is the Lily who helped you, Quinn." He eyed her with curiosity.

"It's a small world," Quinn replied, holding Lily tight to him. "I see you haven't gotten sick."

"I've kept to myself, working long shifts at the hospital. Do you know what's going on?" Blake asked.

Lily listened as Quinn filled Dr. Conrad in.

"I had no idea," Blake said, fascinated. "I thought, hoped, it was something that would blow over. Guess not, huh? Is there anything I can do?"

"No, I don't think so. But if you hear anything let one of us know," Quinn told him.

Blake said goodbye and they parted ways. Lily remained silent as they walked.

"Okay, what was that about?" Quinn asked.

"Ah, you know that jerk doctor I told you about? Well, that was him."

Quinn looked stunned. "You gotta be kidding me," he said.

"I wish I were. I had no idea he was a vamp."

"Sure is. He's a newbie. I think he's been turned five years now. I didn't know he was a doctor."

"Some kind of researcher, actually. A lot of the staff complain about him. I've even seen him stealing bags of blood. Think he drinks it instead of going out to hunt?" Lily asked.

"It's possible. Maybe he has no problem stealing blood here and there to survive. It's a means to an end."

A vampire scientist...

Keeps to himself...

Has his own lab...

"Lily! Earth to Lily," Quinn said, interrupting her thoughts.

"Quinn, could it be Blake?"

Quinn stopped in his tracks. "What?"

"The virus, the disease. Think for a minute. He's got a lab all to himself, and plenty of time on his hands. He might have the ability to create something like this."

Quinn narrowed his eyes. "Why on earth would he do that?"

"I don't know. Maybe he can't adjust to life as a vampire. Hunters have their reasons...maybe he does, too."

"But he's one of us!" Quinn's nostrils flared.

"Humans kill each other every day! Why is it so inconceivable to you that a vampire would turn on his own kind? Maybe he doesn't see things like you and Dimitri do. You have to admit Quinn, it's possible."

Lily watched as Quinn dug the toe of his boot into the ground. Finally, he looked up at her.

"As much as I hate to say it, you're right. It's possible. Come on, we'd better get to Dimitri."

Quinn led Lily to a hidden entrance at the back of the old house where Dimitri lived.

Looking from the outside, anyone would think it was abandoned, as the windows and doors were sealed tight, but unsuspecting humans didn't know that the place was sealed up to prevent a vampire from being fried by the sun.

They walked through Dimitri's home. Quinn flipped on a switch, and the house lit up. Lily followed Quinn closely, looking around as she went. It was elaborately decorated. Plush carpet covered the floors. Rich tapestries hung where the windows would be. Rugs, paintings, and decorations looked as if they had been acquired around the globe.

"Haven't you learned any manners in the past two hundred years? You didn't knock," Dimitri scolded as they entered the living room. He sat in the corner, a beautiful woman on his lap.

"I see you've been...relaxing," Quinn said.

"I needed to unwind a bit. Come, sit. Svetlana, go make yourself busy."

Lily watched the leggy woman exit the room. She could hear movement from deeper inside the house. Lily didn't dare to think how many vampires lived here.

"I expected you here earlier. We need to figure out a new plan."

"We think we may have one," Quinn said. "We need to check out Blake."

"Blake? Why?" Dimitri asked, clearly confused.

Lily piped up. She told Dimitri of how they had run into him and repeated her theory.

"You've proven even more useful than I thought you would be. Let's go check this out," he said. But as Dimitri stood to go, he faltered.

"What is it?" Quinn asked.

"I...don't know." Dimitri grimaced, his pale skin turning gray before reddening. Quinn stood immobilized, while Lily ran into the kitchen. She got back just in time for Dimitri to get sick in the bucket she brought. Quinn watched as the bucket filled with black blood.

"Oh, shit," Lily said, trying not to throw up.

"Go, Quinn!" Dimitri growled, retching. "Tell the others to stay below and not to come up here for anything." Dimitri fell back into his chair, more blood spewing from his mouth.

"And then what?" Quinn asked, full-blown panic rising inside him.

"Check out Blake! If it's him, maybe he can stop this!" Dimitri yelled, and threw up again.

"Go!" Lily echoed. "All you can do is watch him die if you stay." She pushed back the hair from Dimitri's face. If her blood was going to react to the virus, they'd find out soon enough.

"Lily, where is he?" Quinn growled.

"The hospital. There's a back entrance, by the dumpsters. That's the way into his lab. Nobody goes behind there," Lily told him. Her hands shook violently as she held the bucket.

"I'll be back," Quinn said, rushing out. "Just hold on."

Blake returned to his lab, feeling exhilarated, but also slightly annoyed.

"Nigel, things are working even better than I thought!" The rodent scurried around his cage.

Thanks to Quinn, Blake had a more accurate account of what was going on. It was unfortunate though, that the lippy lab tech was Quinn's human.

"Funny though, that Quinn isn't dead," he said, a frown on his face. "I suppose he's just been lucky to not come in contact with it yet. I'm glad he's not dead, Nigel. I learned some valuable information tonight."

He went to his desk and turned on his laptop. He needed to document this new information. The virus had worked as well as, if not better than, he'd expected. Jackson Black's research had predicted the same thing.

"That idiot," Blake whispered as he entered the password on his computer.

Blake learned of Jackson's research several years ago. He'd been so involved with his own studies, he had no idea there was a bounty on his head, until Jackson had caught him with silver chains. As he began to writhe in agony, he had only one option for survival.

"I want vampires dead as much as you do!" he had yelled, catching Jackson off guard.

"What do you mean?" the vampire hunter asked.

"I never wanted to be like this," he spat. "I want them dead as much as you do. I'm on the brink of a virus—"

This grabbed the hunter's attention. He took off the chains as Blake told him of his research. Coincidentally, Jackson Black had been doing similar work.

A rare thing happened that night. A hunter and a vampire called a truce. Working together, the breakthrough had come sooner than they could have hoped.

"But he had to go, Nigel. He fulfilled his purpose." Blake smiled as he began to record the new information Quinn had given him. He had just finished documenting the data when he heard footsteps behind him. Startled, he turned to look behind him.

"Quinn, how did you get in here?"

"I broke the lock," Quinn replied.

"What do you want?" Blake shut off his laptop.

"I needed to see you. To see if you know how to stop this." Quinn wanted to grab him by the neck but restrained himself.

"You mean this sickness?" Blake shifted uneasily, never making eye contact.

If he had to, Quinn planned to tear up the lab to find a cure for Dimitri. He was beginning to lose the little patience he had. "I'm pretty sure that you know more than you're letting on. Dimitri's sick. If you had anything to do with this, I'll kill you myself," Quinn growled, closing in on him.

As Quinn approached, Blake's pallor changed. His skin turned gray as a look of confusion crossed his face. Quinn watched as Blake's face began contorting as he clutched his stomach.

"Oh shit, you've got it!" Quinn cried.

Blake ran past him to the sink on the side wall. He just made it there when he vomited blood into the metal basin, some of it splashing up the sides and onto the floor.

"Did you release more of it tonight?"

Blake nodded yes before heaving into the sink again. He collapsed onto the tile floor. Then he pointed to a cabinet. "Please, in there," he gasped. Quinn followed Blake's gaze and opened the wooden door.

Quinn stared, stunned. Inside were dozens of bottles, all marked 'anti-viral'.

"What's this?" Quinn asked, holding up a bottle to show Blake.

"The cure. It's a nasal spray. Give me one. It's painful, but it works. Please, give me one. Then you can take one for Dimitri." Blake gasped, struggling to get up. The movement did him no good. He gagged, then blood gushed out of his mouth and all over the crisp white lab coat.

"So, you did create this! Why would you do such a thing?" Quinn bellowed, anger taking over.

Blake wiped his mouth, smearing blood on his chin. His skin began to break out with boils.

"I never asked to be like this," Blake spat, letting his fangs extend. "I hate every last one of you. I planned to kill you all, before taking myself down."

"Genocide," said Quinn, disgusted. He wanted to torture this pathetic bastard, rip him into tiny pieces, but he couldn't waste time. Dimitri's life hung by a thread. He had a better idea.

Blake wailed in agony.

Quinn searched the room quickly. In the supply closet he found a garbage bag, which he filled with every last bottle of the anti-viral.

"What...what are you doing?" Blake asked. "Give me one of those!"

Quinn laughed. "Nope, not going to happen. I'd love to tear your head off, but I think this is much more fitting."

"What?" Blake asked.

"I'm going to let you die of your own creation. That's what you get when you mess with things that you shouldn't. It always comes back to bite you in the ass."

Quinn took out a small length of rope from his pocket and tied it around the weakened vampire's wrists.

"I would love to watch you die, but I have more important things to do," Quinn said.

"No! Please don't leave me here!" Blake screamed at Quinn's retreating back.

This was one time Quinn didn't mind letting one of his own kind die. He only hoped he could get back to Dimitri before the same thing happened to his friend.

Lily rinsed a facecloth under cold water, blood coming off her hands. The vomiting had stopped, but Dimitri's skin burned under her touch. She headed back into the bedroom, where she now tended to Dimitri. She had taken off his soiled clothes and kept cold cloths on his forehead. She tried her best not to touch the sores that had broken out over his body.

"Tell Quinn..." Dimitri gasped.

"Listen, whatever Quinn needs to know you can tell him," Lily said sternly. She was trying to be optimistic, but she kept forgetting she was dealing with a vampire who knew he was dying.

"Just tell him, please, that the contents of my safe are his, if he lives through this," Dimitri wheezed.

Lily felt her eyes well. "I will," she promised.

Dimitri closed his eyes and coughed. Lily listened to his ragged breathing.

Lily's stomach felt unsettled and sour. She didn't know if it was the virus or nerves.

She was emerging from the bathroom with another cold cloth when Quinn burst into the room. Relief flooded her body. She watched as he went to Dimitri's side.

"This is going to hurt, but it's gonna make you better," Quinn told Dimitri.

Lily watched as Quinn twisted open a bottle and stuck the tip in Dimitri's nostril. He gave it a good squirt.

"What's that?" Lily asked.

"The cure to this hell. I just hope he's not too far gone." She watched as he opened a bag, taking out several more bottles. "I took every bottle I could find," Quinn explained.

"Was it Blake?" Lily asked.

"Yes. You were right. How are you?" he asked.

"I'm okay."

Quinn looked at her, eyes serious. He took a bottle and put it in her hand.

"I'm all right, Quinn. My stomach's a bit upset, but that's just nerves," she assured him.

He closed his eyes and sighed. "Don't make me do it for you."

She quickly snuffed the liquid. It felt cold as it entered her sinus cavity.

Dimitri let out a groan. "It hurts like hell." He moaned again, and clutched at his stomach.

"Ah, big bad vampire can't handle a little bit of pain?" Lily chided.

"Shut up, witch!"

"You're whining like a baby. You're starting to sound like a human," Lily said. She couldn't resist taunting him, now that it seemed he wasn't going to die after all.

"If you weren't Quinn's favorite plaything, I'd make you pay when this is over," he growled.

Quinn began to say something, but Lily stopped him.

She felt a twinge of pain herself, like a mild headache. But she kept it to herself.

As she looked at the bloody mess on her, she knew she should get a shower, but her adrenaline supply had run out. Lily sat in the wingback chair, while Quinn sat vigil over Dimitri.

The sores on Dimitri began to fade slowly, and his groaning quieted as the night wore on. Lily closed her eyes and slept a broken sleep.

Once when she woke, she saw Quinn taking a bottle for himself. She jumped up, but he stopped her.

"I'll be fine," he said. She watched through slitted eyes as a grimace of pain crossed his face, but he made no sound.

As morning approached, Quinn gently lifted her and carried her to a bed in the adjoining room. He lay beside her, and the last thing she heard before passing out was Quinn whispering his love for her.

Quinn woke, his groggy mind clearing quickly when he found Lily was gone. As he sat up, he noticed a piece of paper next to him.

Be back soon,

Lily

He pocketed the note as he headed to the next room to find his friend already awake.

"How are you feeling?" Quinn asked as he surveyed Dimitri. His skin had almost completely cleared.

"Hungry," he said to Quinn.

A soft knock came from behind them.

"I thought I heard you talking. I have something Dimitri will want."

"I bet she does," he whispered to Quinn, an impish grin on his face. It seemed, for the time being, he had forgotten Lily's taunts from the night before.

Quinn was surprised to see what Lily had.

"Did you murder someone?" he asked, staring at the bags of blood she held.

"Nope, but I went to the hospital and snuck these out. I knew after last night, Dimitri would need it," she said.

"Give it here!" Dimitri commanded.

Quinn watched Lily turn three shades of green when Dimitri's fangs slid out, biting into the bag like it was a juice pack.

"I think I'll wait out here," she said. Quinn noticed Lily had showered and changed.

Quinn waited patiently for Dimitri to drink.

"That's better," Dimitri said, wiping his mouth.

"What happened last night?" he asked Quinn.

Quinn sat beside his friend, filling Dimitri in on the events of the previous night.

"He died a most fitting death. You did the right thing, my friend. I owe you for saving my life."

Quinn looked away. "No, you don't. I think I'll stay here for a night or two, until you're back to your old self."

"I feel too shitty to argue," Dimitri said.

"I'll have to go back to the lab. I need to take Blake's laptop and what's left of the virus. We can't let that get into the wrong hands."

"I agree. Burn him and bring back his ashes, too. I want to put them in an urn before putting it on my mantle."

"Why would you do that?"

"It's a trophy, idiot. Another enemy conquered."

"I should thank you also, Lily," Dimitri said as Lily came back in. "I am in your debt."

"There's no need," Lily said. "I did what I had to do."

"Either way, you may need assistance someday. Know that you can come to me, and I will help," Dimitri told her. "You know, you're pretty nice—for an entrée."

"Well, thanks. I'll remember that. I'm going home. I called off from work. I'd like to have a night of doing nothing, instead of interviewing slayers or taking care of whining vampires," Lily said mischievously.

Dimitri began to say something when Quinn interrupted.

"Okay, troublemaker, I'm taking you home."

Lily laughed at Dimitri's scowling face. She wasn't so afraid of him anymore.

When they reached her apartment, Quinn walked Lily inside.

"Chivalry hasn't died completely, I see," she said.

"Oh, I'm very old-fashioned," Quinn said, and Lily laughed.

"You really are something," he said.

"What do you mean?" she asked.

"You're not faint of heart. Not many humans would handle what you've gone through," he said.

"I'm a tough chick," she told him. "I can cope with you and whatever crazy shit comes along." She smiled and looked up at him.

Quinn looked into her emerald green eyes and knew without a doubt, he loved her.

"That's good," he said, "because I'm not going anywhere. So there's bound to be more 'crazy shit' around the corner."

She laughed, and he bent to kiss her lips.

"Then it's a good thing I'm tough," she said, and pulled him closer.

Harvest

"I don't think this was a good idea after all, Quinn," Lily said, shifting her backpack.

"Trust me, it'll be worth it. If you lifted your feet a little higher, you'd stop tripping," he said.

"If I could see in the dark like you, I wouldn't be having that problem."

An owl hooted, startling Lily, and she fell onto the mossy forest floor.

"Crap!"

Quinn's strong arms lifted her up and onto his back.

"I'd like my mere mortal to survive this trip," he teased, as she tightened her arms and legs around his broad back.

"Ha-ha."

In the few months she had known Quinn, Lily had not only saved his life but also had helped catch vampire hunters. Quinn told Lily that she'd earned a well-deserved vacation, so he rented a cabin, far from the city away from bad memories.

Lily inhaled deeply, taking in Quinn's scent. Smells pretty good for a vampire. He smelled of old books and rooms left forgotten. His shaggy brown hair tickled her face.

She felt better than she had in a long time, and knew Quinn did, too. She could feel it radiating from him. When she had been used as bait to trap him, the only way Quinn could save her life was to let Lily drink his blood. It had healed her and left them sharing a bond that would last until death separated them.

"You're happy," he said.

"So are you."

She nuzzled her face into his neck. His skin, although unusually cool to the touch, was soft and smooth. She was no longer leery of her heroic vampire, but intrigued by him.

"Quinn, how does a human become a vampire?"

"Any specific reason you're asking?"

"I'd like to get some facts straight. I deserve to know the truth."

"The night you drank my blood would have been the perfect opportunity for me to turn you, if I'd wanted to," Quinn said bluntly. "All I had to do was drink from you at the same time you drank from me."

"Oh, are people willing?"

"We have...ways of getting humans to comply. Look, Lily, I told you we were close," he said, pointing ahead.

They entered a small clearing. Moonlight pierced the darkness. In the distance a brook babbled softly. She looked up at the clear night sky, full of glittering stars.

"It's beautiful! Okay, let me down." Lily loosened her grip on Quinn's neck. But instead, Quinn stood still. Not one muscle in his body twitched.

A tingling sensation washed over her as emotions flooded from him. He was suddenly uneasy. She wrapped her arms around Quinn's neck again, holding tightly.

"Something's not right," he told her, voice low. He peered around the clearing, sniffing the air as he moved.

"Is someone here?" she whispered into his ear.

"Not anymore. It's probably nothing. I'll check things out."

He started to put her down, but Lily refused to move.

"No way, I'm staying with you."

Quinn didn't protest. He began to sniff the air again as he slowly walked through the clearing.

"What do you smell?"

"Something foul. I can't quite tell what it is."

Crickets chirped as Quinn walked slowly through the grass. As they drew closer to the other side, he began to walk faster. Lily gripped tighter as her body bobbed up and down. When Quinn stopped, he shimmied Lily down his body and set her on the ground.

"I need to check that out," he said, pointing to a mound under a tree.

Lily stayed close as his strong fingers worked to dig the dirt. The dampness of the freshly dug earth filled Lily's nostrils.

Lily looked at Quinn as he knelt by the hole. She felt scared and suddenly chilled. The crickets had even stopped chirping.

Just as Lily thought the silence was going to kill her, he said,"Fuck!" Her body began to shiver. It was one thing to know he was angry, it was a whole new ball game when she could feel it. She put a hand on his shoulder as she peered over him and into the hole.

"Did you just dig up a grave?"

Lily stared into the open hole. A brunette woman lay inside. Her arms were crossed, as if someone had taken great care with her. Dried flowers scattered the grave, along with a few items Lily couldn't make out.

"She's a vampire," he replied.

Lily watched as he peeled white lips back from bloodless gums. He pressed on the soft flesh; a fang popped out.

A mixture of frustration and anger washed from his body, hitting Lily with force. She knelt down and took his dirt-caked hands into hers. He looked at her, pain in his eyes.

"I thought when vampires die, they...um..."

"Turn into dust?"

"Yeah."

Quinn shook his head. "More like ashes. But that's only in the sunlight."

A horrible thought flashed through her mind. Quinn stepping into the sun, disintegrating. She shook her head violently to erase the image.

"What is it?" he asked.

"Uh, nothing. What do you make of this?"

"I don't know. I've never seen a vampire buried like this before." Quinn picked up a few items Lily hadn't been able to identify.

"See this? These are bones from a cat, probably a kitten. What really gets me is the heart."

"What heart?"

Quinn placed the bones on the ground and reached into the grave again.

"This is the heart of a bull. It looks as if it's stuffed with herbs."

"How do you know that?"

"Lily, if you've been around as long as I have, you know a lot of useless crap."

"How did she die?"

"I have no idea."

He wrapped his arm around Lily and hugged her tight. "I'll cover her up again, then we'll head back to the cabin. So much for our romantic evening."

Lily stared at her dropped pack. She had brought a blanket for them to lie back on and stargaze.

"What are you going to do about...her?"

"I have a friend I'll call who will help. Pass me your backpack."

Lily grabbed the purple bag and handed it to Quinn. He dug to the bottom of it and pulled out a plastic bag. He gathered the bones, herbs, and flowers from the grave. "He'll know what to make of these," he told her, as he covered the grave.

"I'll make this up to you, I promise," he said as they headed back to the cabin.

"It's okay." She slipped her hand into his.

Sebastian scrubbed the dirt ground beneath his fingernails. The water scalded his skin as he worked furiously. It was the worst part of the whole process: cleaning up.

"Are you sure you put all the ingredients into the body cavity? It's important we find the right spell, Bastian."

He rolled his eyes, grateful the sink faced away from his worrisome wife.

"Don't you think I know that, Claire? We were so close the last time. It won't be long now until we find the exact spell that will regenerate a vampire."

"Okay," Claire said wringing her hands together. "You know how I worry. Now that we have a real cure it's important not to let it slip by us."

Sebastian turned off the water and dried his hands.

"I sometimes wonder if you forget that I am the sangoma here. I know how valuable vampire blood will be to us and our people!"

Claire seemed to shrink. "Yes, you're right. I am sorry, Bastian."

Five years had passed since Sebastian and Claire Dumont had migrated from South Africa to Canada in search of new resources for their clients. Back home, Sebastian was a respected and sought-after healer. Other healers paid him dearly for cures and treatments. The rarer the item needed, the higher the price.

Claire wrapped her arms around him. His irritation evaporated, and he held her close.

"Husband, in the years we have been together I have seen and witnessed much, but the only thing that has truly frightened me are those vile creatures."

"Between my spells and hunting skills, you have nothing to fear."

Only a month ago, Sebastian had learned the full potential of vampire blood. A story had quickly taken root and spread. A woman's life had been saved by drinking the blood of a vampire. He'd heard several versions of the story, but the one thing that never changed was the healing power of the blood. Within days he had formed a plan. He began creating spells to neutralize the undead, allowing him to wrap silver chains around their vulnerable forms. The weakened vampires could then be drained and harvested.

Sebastian pulled away and nodded to the table. "Make sure it's cleaned and prepared. Tomorrow night there'll be another."

"Where did you bury the last one?" she asked.

"What does it matter?"

"Just so I know to stay away. I need to go looking for herbs tomorrow."

"West of here, near the clearing."

She nodded and set out to finish cleaning.

It had been Claire's idea to attempt to preserve the body. After draining and gutting the vampires, a special spell kept them from decaying. Once the body was prepared it was buried, with more spells. They hoped to hit upon one that would cause the body to regenerate, leaving the vampire to be re-harvested.

Sebastian went into his study. On his desk were the newest orders from clients. He picked them up to review the list. He smiled. Once Mr. Edwards paid in full, Sebastian would send him a vial of vampire blood, and his patient would be cancer-free.

He went to the safe and opened it. Stacks of money filled the metal box. His smile widened.

Quinn looked at Lily, who slept peacefully in his arms. The fire burned bright, warming the small cabin. Lily had curled up with him on the sofa while they waited for Eric to arrive. It hadn't taken long before she was snoring softly. He was glad to see her fall asleep after the newest bombshell he'd dropped on her.

"There's something you need to know about Eric," Quinn told her earlier.

"What's that?" she asked as she busied herself making a snack. "Is he another vampire?"

"Nope, definitely not a vampire. He's a werewolf."

"Are you freaking kidding me?" she spouted, crumbs flying from her mouth.

"I need his help, Lily. Besides, you've been hanging out with vampires. I didn't think you'd mind." Quinn felt the rush of fear wash from her. He could see in his mind's eye flashes of what she feared: large rabid dogs.

"Eric is harmless. Trust me. I wouldn't knowingly let anyone or anything that could hurt you nearby."

Lily hadn't seemed entirely convinced, so now Quinn looked forward to their meeting with Eric with some nervousness. Still, she had fallen asleep, so that was a good sign.

His acute hearing picked up the roar of Eric's Mustang a mile away. Despite the circumstances and his worry about Lily, he was looking forward to seeing his old friend.

He bent and kissed Lily on the forehead, gently waking her.

"What's going on?"

"Company's coming."

As the car pulled in the driveway, Lily groaned.

Quinn got up just as there was a knock on the door. He heard Lily's tiny feet pad slowly behind him. The door burst open before Quinn could get to it.

"Quinn, my man! It's been a while!" Eric dropped his bags on the floor before grabbing Quinn in a bear hug. Quinn let out a startled "Oof." Eric was tall, close to Quinn's height. He had short, spiky blond hair and bright, shining emerald green eyes. He wore an old bomber jacket, white tee, and worn jeans.

"So, who's the little lady?" Eric asked, winking at Quinn. A sly grin crossed his face. "Let me guess, you're the chick who saved his punk ass, right?"

Quinn growled slightly. He hated being reminded that he'd let himself get cornered. "Yeah, this is Lily," he said, smiling down at her as he pulled her close.

Eric reached for Lily's hand, kissing the back of it. Quinn felt her nervousness, but she didn't let it show.

"Don't worry darlin'. I won't bite. Unlike Quinn."

"Quinn tells me you two are old friends. How did a vampire and werewolf meet anyway?"

Eric took off his jacket and hung it up. "When my baby sister, Faye, was a kid, she got attacked by a rogue werewolf. Quinn saved her. He followed her scent back to the farm in time for us to fix her up. She'd be dead if he hadn't come along."

Quinn shifted awkwardly. He had only done what was right, and Eric's family still felt indebted to him. They had made him an honorary pack member.

Eric talked to Lily while Quinn scrounged up food for his friend. Eric was a flirt and within minutes Lily was completely at ease.

Note to self, werewolves aren't half bad.

Lily joined the men at the table. She put another beer in front of Eric. "Thanks, sweetheart," he said, smiling.

"So what do you think is going on?" she asked Eric.

He took a swig before answering. "I'd say some kind of black magic. My sis knows a lot about these things. We'll go see her tomorrow."

"Do you think another vampire did this?"

"I don't think so. I could smell human out there," Quinn said. "May have been hikers, but the scent was strong in the earth I dug up."

"I didn't think many humans knew vampires existed," Lily said thoughtfully. "I guess I was wrong."

"Actually Lily, ever since Quinn saved you from Creighton you've been big talk in the supernatural world."

"Why am I big talk?"

Quinn remained silent, but Eric answered her.

"Vampires rarely, and I mean rarely, give their blood to a human unless they're turning them. Every vampire has heard how Creighton was finally bested, and how Quinn saved you in the process. It's taboo for a vamp to do what Quinn did."

"Why?"

"You can shut it now," Quinn said through gritted teeth.

"Because he risked exposing the entire vampire race to the human world. In some cases, vampires who have fed a human their blood have been executed. He risked his ass to save you. But vampires were so happy Creighton was finally dead, that they didn't care about what Quinn did. Nobody thinks of you as a serious risk, anyway. If you tried to expose us, people would just say you were crazy."

Lily sat stunned. Tears welled in her eyes.

Quinn risked his life for me.

"Quinn," she whispered.

"Don't," he replied, his voice gruff.

"So what's the plan then?" she asked, clearing her throat.

"Eric's going to talk to his sister, and you're going with him. If something goes down during the day, he'll protect you. You're as safe with him as you are with me."

"I don't need a bodyguard, Quinn."

"I would like if you two stuck together during the day, just in case something did happen. It's only a precaution."

"I'm sure the last thing Eric wants is to be stuck with me."

"Listen, sweetheart, guarding that body will be the highlight of my life," Eric said, eyes twinkling.

The table suddenly shifted. "Hey! You didn't have to kick me, Quinn."

Lily laughed. "Looks like I have two protectors now."

It was mid-afternoon when Eric woke from his deep slumber.

"It's about time you got up," Lily said, teasingly. She poured them both a cup of freshly brewed coffee.

"Don't rush me, darling," he said, his voice husky. "We've got plenty of time. Besides, you can blame that boyfriend of yours. He's the one who kept me up until dawn." He thanked her for the coffee and sat down at the table.

It was an hour later when Eric was ready to get going. Lily sat in the passenger seat of the muscle car, heading out to begin their investigation.

"So tell me about your sister. How can she help?"

Eric smiled. "You'll like my baby sis. Faye is a hard person not to like. Ever since we were kids, she was fascinated by the supernatural. The boys were just stoked we could do things regular humans couldn't, but Faye wanted to understand it all. She's been reading books on just about every topic you can think of. She was the only girl I knew who asked Santa for books about the occult. She owns a store, so that's where we're heading."

"A store? All the way out here?"

"You haven't been out here before, have you? The main roads are busy most of the year with tourists. In the winter it's mainly locals. She sells books, mostly, but she's always getting in new things."

"Does she know I'm coming and that I know...your secret?" Lily asked. She didn't like the thought of upsetting Eric's sister.

"Everyone in our family knows about you, Lily. I'm sure she will like you, even though you stole Quinn's heart."

Lily blushed. "What does that mean?"

"Faye had a crush on Quinn for years," Eric said, laughing. "She says she's over it, but she still gets all doe-eyed around him." He ate the last of a chocolate bar, crumpled the wrapper, and threw it in the backseat before pulling out another.

Lily really didn't like the idea of being in a love triangle with a werewolf. I hope Faye really is over Quinn.

Lily took in the scenery as they drove. The ocean glistened in the afternoon sunshine. An eagle soared and dove to snatch a fish from the cool water. Majestic trees edged the mountains, towering over the forest creatures. I really have to get out here more often.

Eric pulled the car into a short dirt driveway leading to a small building at the end. The property was neat and well-tended. The store itself looked like an old cabin. A sign that read "All Things Fey" sat above the door. Wind chimes hung from the eaves, the light breeze making them sing softly. In the large picture windows hung sun catchers of every size. Lily had a feeling she was going to spend a mini-fortune.

As Eric opened the door to the shop, chimes tinkled to announce their arrival.

"Be right there!" a woman's voice called.

Along two sides were floor-to-ceiling bookshelves. Multicoloured pillars of candles stood on tables, and a jewelry case sat below the cash register, holding beautiful treasures made from stones, beads, and shells. Lily walked to one of the book-lined walls and ran her fingertips over the bindings. They held a huge variety of topics that Lily wouldn't have thought about until recently. Vampires: Myths And Legends, Aliens and the People They Abduct, Witchcraft for Dummies, and How To Use Rune Stones were some of the titles she saw.

"This is the greatest little store," Lily said to Eric as she looked around.

"She's done a good job," he replied, but Lily took no notice. She was too engrossed.

"Eric!" a voice called, startling Lily. She turned to see a tall, attractive woman come out from behind a beaded curtain. She was blond like Eric, and wore her hair in a messy bun. Stray tendrils framed her face. Her eyes were the same emerald green colour as Eric's. She wore a light pink summer dress that fell to the floor.

"So, it's baby sister to the rescue, is it?"

"I wouldn't say that," Eric said, puffing out his chest. "Faye, this is Lily." Lily smiled brightly and extended her hand. The other woman hesitated for a fraction of a second, then stiffly reached out.

"Finally, I meet the human who saved our Quinn. I have heard much about you."

"Oh, it was nothing," Lily said, still smiling even though she felt slightly uncomfortable. The woman smiled, but her eyes did not.

"Lily, I do hope you understand how important it is to keep this all a secret. Not many humans know the truth, and we like to keep it that way."

"Now Faye, relax. Lily's a smart woman who has been introduced to our world pretty harshly. She isn't about to go off spouting our secrets."

"Well, that's good to hear," Faye replied. "Give me just one moment." Faye went to the door, locked it, and put a "closed" sign in the window.

"We don't need anybody walking in when we're talking about God knows what." She led them to a cozy reading area in the far corner.

"So, what exactly is going on, Lily? Eric tells me you and Quinn found a buried vampire."

Lily filled Faye in on what had happened.

"Huh," Faye said when Lily finished.

"What?" Eric asked.

"I started hunting near there a few weeks ago. I didn't see or smell anything out of the ordinary."

"Well until this gets figured out, you're to stay away from there," Eric said, the protective big brother coming out.

"But—"

"No buts about it. I will skin your hide if you go within ten miles of there."

Faye cleared her throat. "Fine."

Lily realized what was going on between them because Quinn had explained it to her. Eric was not only her brother, but also the alpha male of their family. Faye had no choice in the matter.

"All right, so what exactly was in the grave?"

Lily pulled out the bag and emptied the contents onto the small coffee table between them. "There was also a bull's heart, but we left that behind."

She watched as Faye picked up the flowers, herbs, and bones to study them. They sat quietly as Faye got up to retrieve a book and finger through it.

"Just what I was afraid of," Faye said as she closed the book. "Kinda makes sense. If this is what I think it is, we all have to tread carefully."

"What?" Lily and Eric both asked.

"I'm pretty sure we're dealing with a sangoma."

"What the heck is that?" Lily asked.

"A shaman or medicine man, or what some might call a witch doctor," Faye explained.

"What would a witch doctor be doing around here?" Lily found the explanation crazy.

"Sangomas have long believed that albinos held special healing power," Faye said slowly. "They often use tissues, blood, and organs in healing spells. It comes at an extremely high price for the client. It's possible—although I never made the connection before—that vampires, with their paler skin, were the 'albinos' they hunted all along."

"Huh," Eric said.

"If not," Faye continued, "there is the possibility that they have learned of vampires and exactly what their blood can do." She shot a dark look at Lily. "Hence the drained and hollowed-out body. The items were part of a spell, one of rejuvenation, I think. It's possible that whoever did this hoped to regrow the vampire's organs, allowing the body to be harvested again."

Lily blanched. *That is truly vile.*

"You okay?" Eric asked.

"Yep." Lily swallowed. "So, how does he capture the vamps? It wouldn't be easy to outwit them."

"Witch doctors are very skilled. My guess is that he is somehow using a spell or hex to trap them. Some sangomas are said to have great powers."

"Maybe you should stay with my sister until this blows over," Eric said to Lily. A grimace quickly appeared on Faye's lips and vanished just as fast.

"Like hell I am," Lily said defiantly. "No offense, Faye. But I've been through too much with Quinn to sit back."

"No offense taken," Faye said.

"Fine," Eric said.

"Good. Now that that's settled, I'd like to shop," Lily said. "I'm due for some good retail therapy."

Sebastian made his way through the forest, careful not to disturb the area. If vampires knew there were humans nearby, they would either find and kill Sebastian and his wife or flee. He didn't like either choice. Although he had warded their property from detection, there was always the possibility a strong vampire could penetrate them. Sebastian didn't know enough about them to be sure. But he was learning a lot, and fast. Often when he was draining a vampire, they would beg for their life. Sebastian would tell them if they gave him the information he wanted, he would let them live. Of course, that was a lie. After the vampire was drained and harvested, he would write in his journal all the new information he'd learned. He already had two thick journals filled, and he was excited to start his third.

He entered the small clearing and knew instantly something was amiss. Someone has been here.

He listened for any sound of someone close by. When he was sure it was safe, he walked into the clearing.

He edged his way to where he had buried his latest victim, and stopped in his tracks when he saw that the mound under the tree had been disturbed.

"What the hell?" As he dug up the grave, he discovered that some of the special items had been removed. The smell of decay pierced his nostrils. The body had begun to rot.

Even though he was rattled that his prize had been discovered, he needed to know if the vampire's organs had regenerated. He lifted her shirt to reveal the abdomen. With shaking hands, he took his knife from its sheath on his belt and ripped the stitches open. He pulled the flesh apart to look inside the body cavity. It was empty.

"Fuck!" he yelled, forgetting to be quiet. He let out a howl of pure rage. With the magical components gone, the body was useless.

Sebastian's hopes had been high. If they had been able to regenerate organs, they could have had a sustainable supply.

The wind picked up, making the branches sway. As they did, a stray beam of sunlight hit the once-beautiful vampire. Instantly, her body began to flake into pieces of ash. Sebastian tried to cover her, but it was too late. She was gone.

He cried out again, his body shaking uncontrollably.

Claire, gathering leaves and herbs far from where her husband knelt, heard his howl and shook her head. "I do not wish to see you anytime soon, husband."

When Quinn woke he heard Lily asking Eric all sorts of questions. The soft flutter of pages accompanied the sound of her voice.

"Are fairies real?"

"I'm not about to go off telling you what else exists," Eric replied.

"Okay, well, can werewolves really only be killed by silver, like vampires?"

"No. I'm mortal like everyone else. I can heal fast, though. Not as fast as that lucky blood-sucking son-of-a-bitch."

Quinn stifled a laugh. When he entered the living room he found Lily sitting on the floor in front of a fire, engrossed in reading. She sat with books and bags scattered on the floor around her. Supernatural For Dummies sat open in her lap.

"Shopping at Faye's, were you?" he asked as he knelt down to kiss her.

"Yup," she replied, looking up at Quinn and smiling. She took out a small velvet bag and tipped it to empty its contents into her delicate hand.

"What's that?" he asked, as she put it into his hand.

"A crystal. This one is for protection. Figured you need all the help you can get." She beamed up at him. He didn't tell her he didn't believe in crystals. Hell would freeze over before he would hurt her feelings. "Thanks," he said, before kissing her.

Quinn looked at Eric, who was coming with a fresh cup of hot coffee and a sandwich. As he sat on the worn sofa, Quinn noticed the playful side was gone. His forehead crinkled, his brows drawn together.

"What does Faye think?" Quinn asked.

"Witch doctor," Eric replied.

Quinn snickered. "Are you for real? I've never heard of any around here."

They both filled Quinn in on what happened that afternoon.

"Great. This is going to prove more difficult than I thought."

"How's that?" Lily asked.

"A sangoma means spells and wards. I have nothing in defense of that. This crystal won't do the trick."

"If you're worried, I guess there's nothing I can do to help," Lily said.

"I don't know about that," said Eric.

Quinn swivelled to look at Eric. "What?"

"I thought you were against me helping!" Lily exclaimed.

"I was, but I've been thinking. You drank Quinn's blood once before, right? Well, if you drank more, it should give you the supernatural advantage, but you'd still be human enough that any wards tuned to vampires would be null against you. You'd allow us to get closer to them."

Quinn glared at Eric. "I'm trying to protect her, not put her in the middle of this."

"I know you're pissed, man," Eric said. "But think about it. If she gets hurt, she'll heal up quickly. Plus she's going to have some of that strength and speed of yours."

I hate admitting when that ass is right.

Quinn looked down at Lily. "The only way you're helping us is if you drink my blood again. Can you handle that?"

Lily moved her purchases aside and got up to stand in front of Quinn, her head held high. "Yes."

Son-of-a-bitch. She loves me. Quinn could feel it coming from her. He had once thought he felt it, now he knew for sure. This little spitfire loved him.

"What?" she asked.

"Uh, nothing. Let's head out now. We are going to find whoever is doing this, and put a stop to it."

Lily once again found herself traipsing through the dark forest. When they reached the clearing, Eric picked up a fresh scent, so he scouted ahead while she walked with Quinn.

She swallowed back a gag as she thought about having to drink blood again, but she knew she had to do it. Quinn had become the most important person in her life.

"You all right with this?"

"Of course," she replied. When she looked up at him he had a funny grin on his face. "What?" she asked.

"Nothing. Listen, we should stop here. I think it's time. If we get ambushed you need to be prepared. Ready?"

Lily nodded. She took a deep breath. "Ready."

Quinn's fangs extended and he pierced his flesh. He withdrew, licking his blood-stained lips. Blood welled from the punctures. "Quickly."

Lily closed her hands on his wrist, and leaned down to put her mouth on the open wound. She gulped mouthfuls of the tangy, sticky fluid. Even as she drank, she felt his wound slowly closing.

"That's enough." He dabbed the red droplets on her mouth.

Lily ran her tongue over the spot where Quinn's fingertips had touched her. Her skin began to tingle. Her body felt hot as power surged through it. Her veins throbbed from an untapped energy.

"I don't remember feeling like this the first time." She felt as if she could conquer the world as power flowed in her veins.

"That's because last time you were at death's door."

Lily could hear the crunching of leaves. She looked around, trying to find the source.

"Your senses are heightened. It'll take you a few minutes to get used to it."

Within moments, Lily saw the silhouette of an extremely large dog coming straight for them.

"Quinn!" Lily moved beside him, preparing for an attack.

Quinn gripped her wrist. "Easy. It's only Eric."

Lily looked again. Big green eyes sparkled.

Eric, in wolf form, slowed his pace and trotted up to them. He was massive. Long fangs extended from his jaw. His paws were the size of baseball gloves. He nuzzled Lily's hand. She gingerly touched the top of his head, petting the coarse brown fur. His eyes glittered in amusement. He barked, startling Lily.

"I think he likes showing off to a human," Quinn said.

Eric sat up to his full height, lifting his head as if to say, "Don't I rock?"

"Find anything?" Quinn asked.

Eric yelped and nodded his head.

"Come on, we'll follow him."

"You can speak wolf?" she asked.

Quinn laughed. "Not exactly. We have our own way to communicate. Body language and the tone of his bark."

Eric began to run, and so did Quinn. "Come on, Lily."

Lily ran, feeling as if there were springs in her legs. The cool night air brushed her face as she sped along. Heightened vision allowed her to avoid each branch instead of getting hit in the face.

This is fantastic!

The vampire blood gave her exhilarating speed.

They ran several miles before the wolf stopped abruptly. Lily wasn't even out of breath. Eric nodded his head as Lily and Quinn came up beside him. They all hunkered down in the brush.

A small cabin sat amongst the trees. Lily smelled the smoke wafting from the chimney. Light shone from tiny windows, and wind chimes clinked in the breeze. She grimaced when she realized they were made out of bones.

Quinn nudged her and pointed to the windowsill. "See those bags?"

She nodded.

"I'm pretty sure that's a hex bag. A spell. And there's more than one of them."

"What kind of spell?" Lily asked.

"Could be wards. Protection spell, possibly."

Lily looked into the cabin, where the outline of a woman showed behind the window. She was looking around frantically.

"What now, Quinn?"

"Stay here with Eric. I'm going to go check something out."

"I can handle myself. I have your blood in me, after all."

Eric growled.

"Shh, something's coming."

Lily's new-found hearing picked up sticks breaking and leaves crunching under a heavy weight. Whatever it was, it was coming fast. Eric stood up on all fours and turned behind Lily. He barked. After a moment, that bark was answered with a howl.

"Faye," Quinn said.

Lily turned around. Faye in wolf form was big, but didn't have Eric's mass. Her fur was honey blond, and her green eyes sparkled.

The two wolves stared at each other for a long moment before Eric snapped at his sister.

"Eric's pissed Faye disobeyed him. Faye said we need all the power we can get," Quinn told her, as Lily watched in awe. Faye sat on her haunches.

Guess she's staying.

"Okay, if we are going to do this, we have to act now. Faye, stay here with Lily."

Faye looked at Lily and narrowed her eyes before nodding at Quinn.

Lily watched Quinn and Eric disappear into the trees. Faye moved to sit beside her. She snorted.

"Don't be upset with me. I told Quinn I didn't need a babysitter." Faye huffed again and turned her head towards the cabin just as the small door suddenly swung open.

A woman burst out, carrying a cross in her hand. "I know you're out there, devils! I can smell you!" she spat out.

Lily noticed the woman's body trembling. "Why on earth would she come out like this?"

Faye let out a low groan and stared off into the distance.

"I get it. She's alone and scared, isn't she? That's why Quinn went out there, he smelled someone else."

Faye looked over at her and nodded.

The woman began to chant in a language Lily had never heard before. Lily had no idea what she was saying, but she was smart enough to know it wasn't an invitation to tea.

She stood and took a step forward. Faye's teeth nipped at her jeans to stop her, but, full of bravado, Lily edged closer. Part of her screamed, Back the fuck up, while the other part yelled, Get the bitch!

She stopped when the woman saw her, and put her hands on her hips. "I don't know what you're doing, lady, but it's not working."

Quinn sped through the woods, Eric on his heels. He caught the scent of the man when the wind shifted. It was the same faint scent he had caught at the burial site.

There he is.

It was the witch doctor, all right. He wore a large headpiece and a bone necklace.

You're mine.

Quinn closed in on his target. He smelled the stench of death on the man. He extended his fangs, preparing for a battle that was sure to end quickly.

But as Quinn approached, he began to slow. His arms and legs felt stiff and heavy. Meters away from his opponent, he couldn't move at all. He stood frozen in place. Eric stopped beside him and barked. Quinn used all the strength in his powerful body to move, but didn't budge. He couldn't even blink. The witch doctor spun on his feet and laughed. Eric lunged, but the witch doctor raised a hand and blew white powder into the werewolf's face.

Quinn heard Eric whimper, but could not turn to look at him no matter how hard he tried. From the corner of his eye, he saw the great beast shake his head, and fall to the ground.

The man let out a cackling laugh. "You belong to me now. Try as you might, undead one, you will not move. Your body is frozen in place. And your furry friend is immobilized."

In the distance, Quinn heard a woman chanting in a strange tongue.

"What have you done to my wife?" the sangoma demanded.

Like I could answer, you dumbass.

Quinn kept straining to move, but it was useless.

"I put traps for dead walkers in this area," he said, pointing around the small clearing.

Quinn cursed himself. He watched as the sangoma walked behind a nearby tree and brought out a large cloth bag. He tipped the contents onto the damp earth. Silver chains rattled as they hit the ground.

Quinn's skin began to itch as old memories resurfaced. He remembered all too well the feeling of the silver chains searing his flesh.

As the sangoma bent to retrieve the chains, he let out a deep laugh.

"You think you're so powerful, undead one. But your kind are no match for my powers. I've killed many of your brethren." He held the chains in his hands and edged forward. Quinn could do nothing but stare in horror. "Your life's blood will serve a higher purpose. It will save many lives, so you will not die in vain."

Eric let out a howl and staggered out in front of Quinn. The witch doctor laughed. "Dog, you are no match for me."

Eric snarled and shook his massive head. He looked at the sangoma for a long moment before leaping up into the air. Quinn watched in helpless horror as the witch doctor unsheathed a blade at his hip, and extended his arm.

Whatever the man had done to Eric, the effect hadn't completely worn off. Eric's aim was terrible. When he jumped, the witch doctor easily ducked and struck out. The blade made a sickening squish as it pierced the werewolf's belly. Eric let out a great howl. Quinn vibrated with anger, but it was not enough to break the spell that held him. He looked at the wolf, who lay on his side. Blood oozed from the wound, into his matted fur and onto the ground. The werewolf whimpered.

I will rip you apart, limb from bloody limb.

"Damn dog made me drop my chains," the man said, as he bent to pick them up from the ground. "Now, where were we?"

Lily sat on top of the woman, holding both her wrists in one hand.

This feels...exhilarating.

The strength that flowed in Lily's veins astounded her. When they had heard Eric's yelp, it distracted Claire, so that Lily was able to pounce on the woman, keeping her trapped beneath her.

Faye growled deeply.

"Why are you doing this?"

"Get off of me, you bitch!"

Lily pushed her face into the dirt. A howl pierced through the night.

What the hell is happening?

Faye whimpered and stared into the woods.

"That's it," Lily said as she stood up, hauling the woman to her feet as if she were a feather. As Lily began to walk into the small home, the were followed her.

Lily ignored the woman as she cried and struggled.

They entered the cabin. A strange smell hit her nostrils.

"Faye, can you help me? I need to tie her up."

The wolf barked, and taking one of the legs of a wooden chair into her jaws, pulled it over to Lily.

"Thanks."

Lily's eyes scanned the room. In the far corner sat a large table with something glinting on top of it. But her attention was drawn to a length of rope hanging on the wall behind it. She pointed it out to Faye, and the wolf retrieved it for her. Within a few moments, Lily had Claire tied snugly to the chair.

"What are you going to do?"

"I'm going to help my friends." Lily's eyes caught sight of the glinting on the table again. This time, Lily went to investigate.

The table turned out to be a workbench.

"Leave it alone!" Claire cried.

The object that had caught her eye was a large knife with a wooden handle.

"What the hell is that?" Lily asked as she bent to look at the table closer. Her nostrils flared. "Blood! This is where he kills them, isn't it?"

The table was stained dark with ingrained blood, as was the handle of the knife. Small saws, knives, and silver chains hung along the wall.

Faye growled.

"You don't understand," Claire cried, tears spilling down her dirt-caked face. "Do you know how many people in my country are dying?" She sobbed, making her body shake. "A vampire's blood can cure our family and friends."

Lily felt for Claire's dying countrymen, but slaughtering vampires wasn't the answer. She listened with enhanced hearing for any sound of Quinn and Eric. "Come on Faye, we gotta go. They should have been back by now. Let's deal with the bitch later."

Faye barked and headed out the door, Lily trailing behind.

Quinn could only let out a muffled cry of pain as he felt the sting of the chains bite into his flesh. The sangoma coiled them around Quinn.

He looked over at his friend, who lay bleeding on the ground.

I should never have brought you into this.

A wolf howled in the distance. Eric lifted his head, but could only yelp a response. It was a direct order to his sister: get the hell out of here.

"Reinforcements? No matter. Your friend won't last much longer, I'm afraid. I have never seen a dog so massive, but he was no match for me. And I will do the same to whatever else shows up here tonight. I am Sebastian, great warrior and sangoma."

Quinn could now smell his own burning flesh. Pain whipped through his body. It felt as if his skin were melting under hot coals. He grew weak, but the spell kept him standing.

If I could only break free, I could still kill this bastard.

Quinn sensed movement coming through the trees straight at them. But the agony of his burning skin, caused Quinn's senses to lose their power. He couldn't tell what, or who, it was.

Behind Sebastian, Quinn watched as a large shadow loomed in the trees. Quinn glanced at Eric. He was motionless.

"Now, let's get you out of here," the witch doctor said.

"Over my dead body!" a voice boomed.

As the shadow edged out, he saw Lily riding upon Faye's back, holding a large knife. Faye snarled.

Sebastian turned from Quinn and reached for his belt, where he had re-sheathed his dagger. Before the man could pull it from its leather holster, Lily lifted the knife she wielded and threw it.

The glinting weapon flew through the air silently and lodged itself in Sebastian's shoulder.

He cried out in pain. "Bitch!" he said, as he clutched the handle.

Faye growled loudly and took a running start at Sebastian. The witch doctor dodged at the last second, and Faye and Lily hurtled toward the thicket of trees behind him. Sebastian wrenched out the knife as Faye spun back towards the man. Lily lost her grip and fell onto the ground. Faye took another run at Sebastian as Lily climbed to her feet.

Sebastian threw the knife, but it sailed past Faye, missing her by inches.

"I curse you!" Sebastian said and began to chant in the same tongue Claire had spoken.

Quinn watched as Faye lifted her large paw into the air and lunged, trying to swipe at the witch doctor. The chanting intensified and he tossed something straight into Faye's eyes. The wolf howled and shook her head. She clumsily took a few steps before falling to her haunches. Faye rubbed her paws frantically over her eyes.

Lily emerged from the thicket. "You smell like the dead one," Sebastian said. "Not quite vampire...not quite human. What are you, woman?"

Lily said nothing as she bent to the ground to pick up the blade Sebastian had thrown at Faye. As she looked about her surroundings, he began chanting again.

Quinn's fangs were distended, a frenzied look frozen upon his handsome face.

This is how he looks when he feeds.

She looked away. Two werewolves were injured, one maybe even dead. It was up to her now.

But what the hell am I going to do? She had a knife—but was she ready to kill a man in cold blood?

The witch doctor chanted faster, his hands moving in a strange sequence of gestures.

Fear pitted like a hot pool in Lily's stomach. Four lives depend on ME. Fuck.

"I can't let you do that," she said. Vampire blood raged inside her.

"How can you stop me?" His voice cut short as Lily suddenly loomed inches from his face. Her fist crunched into his jaw. Sebastian fell backward onto the ground.

"Bitch!" he yelled, scrambling to get on his feet.

"Let them go!" she yelled back.

"Never!"

Lily had no time to think of a plan as the witch doctor lunged towards her. This time he held a small axe. Her new reflexes kicked in, and she dodged him.

A hot sensation ripped up Lily's arm. Looking down, she saw blood seep out from a gash. But she had an edge. Quinn's blood had already started repairing the wound.

Sebastian was trained to fight, but Quinn's blood made her his equal. They fought, scrambling, dodging and lunging. Lily backed into Faye and almost fell.

"Time for this to end," Sebastian said, his breath coming fast.

"I agree," she said. "Give up. Let my friends go."

"Not a chance."

Sebastian lunged at her, swinging his axe. Lily sidestepped away from Faye and swung at him in return with the knife. If she could wound him, get him to drop the axe—

Sebastian dodged her swing, but a massive paw suddenly swiped Sebastian's legs. He pitched forward into Lily. She flung her hands up to shield herself, and almost effortlessly, the knife she held sank deep into Sebastian's neck. She screamed at the same time the witch doctor cried out, his voice trailing into a gurgle. She stared in horror as her hand, clutching the handle, vanished under a sea of blood. She forced her fingers to let go. As Sebastian dropped to the ground, he stared up at her, mouth open in a soundless scream. Then his eyes rolled back.

Lily stared at her crimson hands.

"You did so good," a voice said. But she stood as if in a trance.

I...killed...someone.

Around her, she heard rustling and more voices, but she couldn't seem to move to see what was going on. She stared down at the dead body at her feet.

"Quinn's coming out of the spell," the voice said again.

Lily blinked and turned her head. Faye, back in human form, stood beside her. The whites of her eyes were red and irritated-looking from the sangoma's attack.

"How...how...," Lily stuttered.

Faye pulled her close and hugged her. "It's okay now. You did so well. My vision was blurry, but I could smell him. His biggest mistake was getting near me. Quinn started moving once he was dead. He pulled off those chains pretty quick."

"Quinn...where?"

"He's helping Eric. God, Lily, you really are as awesome as Quinn says." Faye held her tight.

"She's in shock. Don't leave her, Faye."

But Lily could only stare at the hands that had taken someone's life. Her legs weakened, and blackness rolled in.

Lily opened her eyes.

"Our hero awakens."

She turned her head. Eric stood beside her, wearing only a pair of battered jeans. Bandages swathed his torso. Her eyes wandered around. She rested on the softest bed she had ever lain on.

Eric lifted her head gingerly and held a glass of water to her lips. She sipped the cool liquid.

"Where am I?"

"Faye's."

She looked at her hands. They were clean.

"Quinn got you cleaned up."

"I thought you were dead. Who took care of you?"

"We supes have our...ways," he said.

Quinn was beside her then. He bent down and kissed her gently, stroking her face as he did.

"You were amazing!"

"I killed a man." Tears welled in her eyes. "I thought I could restrain him but..."

"Shh, it's okay." He wiped the tears from her cheeks.

"What happened after..."

"Faye went back to the house to check on the woman. She was gone."

Lily's eyes widened. "What?"

"We don't have to worry about her," Eric said. "She's nothing without her husband. No threat to us."

"The sun is rising soon," Quinn told her. "Faye has a spot where I can spend the day. She will be here, and so will Eric if you need them. You really need to rest."

Faye entered the room, carrying a mug. Her eyes were still red, but not as bloodshot as they had been. "Here, Lily, drink this. It will help you sleep."

Lily felt soft kisses as she drifted off to sleep, the horror of the night fading.

"Now, this is more like it," Quinn said to Lily as he pulled her close. He smiled as she snuggled into him. Quinn was determined to give Lily the romantic getaway he'd intended. After all she'd been through, he planned to make every night as good as possible.

"This is nice," she said. They were curled up in a sleeping bag close to a campfire, the stars winking above them.

"Wait until you see what I have planned for tomorrow night."

She smiled up at him. It was the first time she'd smiled since killing Sebastian.

"Well, you deserve to be treated like a queen. More wine?"

Lily giggled. It was the best sound he'd heard all night.

"I love you. I know that this is crazy, but damn it, baby, I love you. I'll do anything to make you happy."

Lily looked up at him. "I love you, too."

He kissed her then, passionately, trying to convey everything he felt for her.

"But what about...our future? Someday I'm going to die—"

Quinn silenced her with another kiss. When he pulled away, he put his hand on her face and looked deep into her eyes. "Let's not worry about tomorrow. Let's just enjoy each moment. The future will figure itself out." He traced her lips with his fingertips, before kissing her again.

They stayed like that until dawn approached, forcing them to retreat to the confines of the cabin.

Fever

Lily followed Quinn into the farmhouse.

"Happy one hundred and twentieth birthday, old man!" Quinn's best friend Dimitri said, hugging him. Dimitri, the head of all the vampires in the area, had insisted on hosting a little party.

Lily scanned the room. Quinn's friends, the werewolf siblings, were already here. Eric sat in a bean bag chair, holding a beer and scarfing down a burger. His sister, Faye, stood close by. She held a wine glass and was talking to a woman dressed in flowing black clothes, whose dark hair hung in messy curls. The woman had olive skin and looked both exotic and familiar.

"Hey Quinn, who is that?" Lily asked, pointing to the woman. She still wasn't familiar with everyone in the vampire's social circles.

"Gabrielle, but everyone calls her Gabby. She's a witch."

Lily nodded. She remembered now. She'd seen Gabby in a picture with Faye at the werewolf's shop. Faye said that she was an old friend and would be inviting her to the party. She hadn't mentioned what made her "super" at the time so Lily had assumed she was a werewolf too.

A tall man sat in the corner. Lily had a hard time taking her eyes off him. He was thick and muscular. He wore no shirt, a blue and black kilt, and black leather boots. Dark brown curls spilled onto his shoulders. Lily watched as the man stood and walked towards them. He was at least seven feet tall.

"Well, Quinn, 'tis been awhile," he said, with a thick Scottish accent.

"Indeed it has. How have you been, Gareth?"

"Well, as usual. This must be the infamous Lily." He took her hand and kissed the top of it. "'Tis a pleasure to meet you."

"Nice to meet you as well."

"I have lived a long time, lass, and 'tis been a long time since I have seen beauty such as yours."

Lily felt her face redden.

"Are you a vampire as well?" she asked.

"Nae, just your run-of-the-mill immortal highlander," he replied, winking at her.

"Move over, big boy," a woman said. It was Gabby.

"Go chat with the men and leave us ladies, bloodsucker," she said.

Quinn laughed, then bent and kissed her on the cheek. "A pleasure as always, Gabby. I'll be over there," he said, pointing toward Eric.

As Quinn and Gareth walked away, the witch turned towards Lily.

"Finally! I've been waiting a long time to meet you," she said pleasantly and embraced Lily in a hug.

"It's nice to meet you as well. I've only met a handful of Quinn's friends so far."

"Yes, well, I'm glad they had this little shindig. It's a small crowd, but it's better this way. Often, so many kinds of supernatural beings don't get along so well, but we are the few that intermingle. They are all good people and allies. So, tell me, how did you save not one, but two big bad vampires?"

Both Quinn and Dimitri overheard and gave Gabby sidelong glances. They hated being reminded that a human had saved them. And on more than one occasion, to boot.

"It's a long story," Lily said.

"So, you and Quinn are an item now, huh?"

"Yeah. He's really sweet. A great guy."

"That he is," Gabby said. "A vampire, yes, but someone's eating habits shouldn't interfere with a relationship."

"How could I resist him? He's dazzling, pale, and mysterious," Lily said with a smile.

Quinn, who had what looked like a glass of blood in his hand, yelled, "Don't you dare say I sparkle!" This sent the two women into hysterics.

Lily chatted with everyone and ate until she thought she was going to burst. There was enough food to feed an army. She danced with Quinn and knew he was happy. She could feel it, thanks to their blood bond.

"You know what we should do?" Gabby said as she turned down the music. "Let's have a little game of truth or dare."

Eric groaned. "I hate that game."

"I didn't mean the human version. We can take it easy on Lily, though"

"What do you mean?" Lily asked.

Dimitri piped up. "It's not just a regular game of truth or dare. This is a supernatural version. It tends to get interesting."

"This is Quinn's birthday, not yours," Faye said. "Maybe he doesn't want to play."

"Sounds fun to me," Quinn said.

"I don't know if the lass could handle it," Gareth said.

Lily scoffed. "Excuse me, but I survived being vampire bait, helped catch a couple of bad guys, dealt with a vamp virus, and you wonder if I could handle a game of truth or dare? I say bring it on."

Gareth laughed. "She is full of spirit."

"Perfect," Gabby said. "Everyone get comfy."

They formed a circle on the floor. Dimitri took the bean bag chair, while others grabbed big pillows from the sofa. The lights dimmed and candles were lit. The fireplace glowed a faint purple from a spell Gabby used.

"Reach into the bag and pull out a stone," she said to Lily.

Lily's fingers brushed the soft leather bag as she did so.

She looked at the stone. "It says five."

"Then you will go fifth. Pass the bag," Gabby instructed.

Lily handed it to Quinn, who sat on her right. "Three."

Faye took the bag and reached in. "Four."

Dimitri was next. "One."

Then, Gabby. "Seven."

Gareth took the pouch. "Six"

"I wonder what number I got," Eric said sarcastically, as he reached in. "Two."

"Whenever you're ready," Gabby said to Dimitri.

"Quinn, truth or dare?" Dimitri asked.

"Dare."

Dimitri smirked. A shiver ran down Lily's spine. She hated that look on his face. She and Dimitri had made an uneasy peace, but you never knew what was going on in that mind of his.

"Quinn, I dare you to feed some of your blood to Lily. She's done it before, she can do it again."

"Doesn't seem like much of a dare," Gabby said.

"Oh, on the contrary. You see, each time Lily drinks from Quinn, their blood bond gets deeper. The deeper their bond gets, the stronger the connection. A stronger bond means they will eventually be able to read each other's thoughts."

Lily looked up at Quinn. "You don't have to," he told her.

"I know." Lily thought for a minute. She had already developed a bond with Quinn on many levels. She loved him deeply. "I'll do it," she said, "but what if you don't like the changes?"

"I wouldn't have a problem with it." He held her hand.

"So, are you going to do it or not?" Dimitri asked.

Quinn's fangs slid out, and he held his wrist to his mouth.

"You sure?" "Yes," she said.

He sunk his fangs into his flesh. Lily watched blood ooze out from the wounds as he held his wrist out to her. She gently took his arm, put her lips to his skin, and swallowed a mouthful of blood.

"That lass has a strong stomach," Gareth said, grimacing.

"Oh, like you don't," Eric said.

"It is one thing to cause or witness bloodshed. It is a whole new thing to actually drink the stuff. Good going, lass."

Lily grabbed a napkin to dab at her lips. The grin she formed for Gareth faltered as a wave of heat washed over her. She glanced down at the bloody napkin in her hand. It wavered slightly as perspiration broke out on her forehead and on the nape of her neck.

"Lily?" Quinn said, his voice edged with concern.

Lily glanced up at him, but he wasn't even looking at her. He was deep in conversation with Eric. Confused, she shook her head, folded the napkin, and used it to pat the sweat on her forehead, which had begun to drip from her hairline.

"Lily," Quinn whispered as he gently sponged her brow. Her eyelids remained closed, her eyes twitching beneath them. "She's not getting any better," Quinn said, looking over at Dimitri.

"You fed her your blood, didn't you?" he asked.

"Yes, hours ago. It should have worked right away...I don't understand."

Quinn was frustrated. And scared. It wasn't often he felt this vulnerable. This...human. He looked down at Lily, whose fever continued to spike. Her face was flushed.

When he'd visited the night before, Lily had said she wasn't feeling well. She had tried to work up the energy to talk about his upcoming birthday and he'd played along because it seemed really important to her that they do something special. But she just couldn't focus. She had a slight fever, so she took some Advil and lay down to get some rest. She fell asleep in his arms before too long. He stayed with her as long as he could, but when dawn approached he left quietly, not wanting to disturb her. He figured by the time he got back she would be feeling better.

But she wasn't. She was worse. When Quinn returned, he found her still in bed, and after a quick look around he could tell she hadn't gotten up since the night before. Everything in her apartment was exactly the same, nothing touched.

Duke, the tabby cat, meowed loudly. Quinn fed him and went back to Lily's side. Her skin burned under his fingertips. That was when he called Dimitri.

Dimitri sat in the corner chair, legs crossed. "Our blood heals. If all she had was the flu, she should have been better by now. Hell, she should be bright-eyed and ready to go, not still..." Dimitri trailed off. He had a look of concern on his face. That made Quinn cringe. Dimitri rarely showed any worry.

"I know. I dread dawn. I can't just leave her alone all day. What if..."

"Call Faye," Dimitri said. "She'd do anything for you."

Quinn had been an honorary pack member since he'd rescued Faye when she was a teenager. Her brother Eric was one of his closest friends. He knew Faye had nursed a crush on him ever since. They had been through a lot together over the years, and he loved her as if she were his sister.

He dialed her number. After several rings he heard a groggy "Hello?"

"Hey, Faye."

"Quinn," Faye said, suddenly sounding brighter. "How are you doing?"

"I'm...okay. Listen, I need your help."

"What's wrong?" Faye asked. Her tone deepened with concern.

Quinn filled her in on Lily's condition.

"So you need me to look after her while you're down for the day."

"I'm sorry. I know it sounds like playing nurse, but I really am worried. My blood isn't helping her, so I don't think a hospital would, either."

"It's okay. I'll bring some of my books on healing. I'll be there before daybreak."

They said goodbye and hung up.

"Told you she'd do it," Dimitri said.

In the hours that passed, Quinn kept cold washcloths on Lily's face and neck, stroked her hair, tried to get her to eat. He got her to take a little more of his blood, but it still had no effect on the illness.

"Remember the other effects your blood will have," Dimitri warned.

"What do you mean?"

"You know damn well what I mean. The more of your blood she drinks, the stronger your bond will grow. It won't be long now before she will be able to start reading your thoughts."

Quinn didn't know how she was going to react. Frankly, he didn't care. Whatever was wrong with her was scaring the hell out of him, and he would do whatever it took to help her. Even if it meant she was going to be pissed afterward.

"Looks like it's my turn." Eric scanned the group, and his eyes landed on Lily. "Truth or Dare?"

"Truth."

"The night you first met Quinn is when you rescued him from the alley. If you had known he was a vampire before you removed the silver chains from him, would you have still saved him?"

"Like she's going to say she wouldn't have," Faye said.

"Actually, she can't lie. None of you can. The stones had a truth spell put onto them. It will only last the duration of the game," Gabby said, a grin on her face.

Lily looked up into Quinn's eyes. "I would have saved him regardless," she said. "Satisfied, Eric?"

He smiled. "Yup. Quinn, your turn."

"Dimitri. Which will it be?" Quinn asked.

"Dare."

"Are you sure?"

"Why wouldn't I be? I can handle whatever dare you throw at me."

"Okay then. I dare you to drink some of Eric's blood."

"Sure, serve me up on a silver platter, you bastard," Eric said, and grunted.

Quinn laughed. "We take a shot glass, put a bit of your blood into it, and Dimitri downs it. No sweat, eh Dimitri?"

Dimitri scowled, while the rest laughed.

"What's so funny?" Lily asked.

"Dimitri says werewolves smell like dogs and taste revolting," Quinn told her.

"To which I take offense," Eric said, but betrayed his lie by snickering.

"I will do it. But don't drop any fleas in it," Dimitri said.

Eric flipped Dimitri the bird.

Gabby snapped her fingers and a shot glass appeared. Eric grinned as he took it. "Bet he doesn't drink it," Eric said.

They watched as Eric nicked his forearm with his pocket knife, and let the blood drip into the small glass. Lily covered her nose, but the tangy aroma of the blood hit her nostrils anyway. Each time she had tasted Quinn's blood, all her senses heightened for the next few days.

Eric passed the shot glass to Dimitri. The vampire took the glass, held it up, and looked at it with disgust. "Smells foul."

"No, it doesn't," Quinn said.

Dimitri lifted the glass to his lips and tipped back the mouthful of blood. He swallowed it and grimaced.

Quinn burst out laughing. "You've become a bit of a food snob in your old age."

"Oh, and you haven't?"

"I don't murder. That's not being a snob."

Another look of disgust came over Dimitri's face. "Damn it Eric, what the hell do you eat?" Dimitri covered his mouth and gagged.

Quinn laughed even harder.

"What the hell? I don't taste that bad," Eric said, clearly offended that a vampire had just gagged on his blood. "Least I know you won't come looking for me when you get hungry."

"I can't even begin to put into words what you taste like," Dimitri said, and tossed the shot glass into the purple flames. The glass hit the back of the fireplace, shattered, and tinkled into the fire. The heating glass cracked and popped. "And if you ever make me do something like that again, you will rue the day that we ever met."

A cat meowed, startling Lily. It was odd for Dimitri to have a cat around. He referred to her cat as an 'overgrown rat.' Must be a stray hanging around outside.

"Now that we have that little mess over with," Dimitri said, glaring in Quinn's direction, "who is next on the list?"

"My turn," Faye said. "Eric, pick your poison."

"Truth," Eric said.

"What's the worst thing you have eaten while in wolf form?"

Eric turned a shade of green. "Well, one winter back when I was a teenager, I travelled farther than I should have. A snowstorm came up. Even with my enhanced vision, I couldn't see anything but snow. As the night passed I got so hungry that had a human come up, they would have been dinner. Finally, I found a cave and smelled...something...inside it. I found..." Eric trailed off.

"What?" Gabby asked.

"A dead bear, rotten and full of maggots. I ate it like it was a Thanksgiving feast."

Everyone was silent. Lily's stomach churned.

"I had to eat. It was that or starve," Eric said defensively.

"And you kiss women with that mouth," Gareth said, making everyone laugh. "Looks like I'm next. Faye, truth or dare."

"Dare," she said.

"Why don't you show everyone your new trick?" Eric said.

Faye glared at her brother. "You know I wanted to keep that secret, just for a little while. Until I, you know, get it down pat."

"Oh come on, Faye. Show us," Gabby urged.

Faye sighed. "Well, the thing is, a lot of people don't realize that when werewolves change, it's into their full form. But there are some of us who can develop a rare skill."

Faye rolled her sleeves up and lifted her hands for everyone to see. She closed her eyes, brows furrowed in concentration.

The air around Faye shimmered and her hands began to grow, her fingers elongating. Her nails lengthened to seven inches long, sharp as knives.

Lily watched in amazement. Faye was still her human self, but she had managed to shift her hands into a large set of deadly claws.

"That is epic!" Quinn said.

He was right. Lily knew that was impressive. She began to feel boring. What could she offer Quinn? She couldn't protect him with claws, or wow him with something supernatural. One time she had to drink his blood to give her strength so she could protect herself. She felt mildly pathetic, as if she did not fit in with them.

I don't belong. That's why.

Quinn turned his head towards her, eyes narrowed.

You belong with me.

Lily gasped. Quinn had heard her thoughts.

She turned back to Faye. Her hands were back to normal, dainty human ones.

Eric patted her on the back. "I'm jealous," he said.

"You should be," Dimitri said. "She's got the looks and the talent in the family."

"Oh, haha," Eric quipped back.

That would be so cool, to be able to have an ability like that. Lily couldn't help but feel a green-eyed monster eat at the back of her mind. I hate feeling jealous.

Quinn looked at her and she heard: Well, that's only fair since Faye is jealous of you.

The doorbell rang. Quinn ran out to get it. "Thank God you're here," he said, enveloping Faye in a hug.

"How is she? Any change?"

"No, still the same."

They walked through the townhouse to the bedroom. Lily murmured in her sleep.

"Nice to see you, Faye," Dimitri said.

"Wow. No dog insults?"

"No, not tonight. I think Quinn would rip my head off if I made one misstep tonight."

Faye walked over and put a hand on Lily's forehead. "She's burning up."

"I know."

"I'll do all I can, Quinn. But there has to be more to this than a regular flu. If your blood has done nothing for her..."

"What do you think it is?"

"I don't know, but I'll help you figure this out. I brought some things from my store. I called Gabby, too, for ideas. Hope you don't mind."

Quinn shook his head. Lily needed any help she could get.

Faye had a vast knowledge of the occult. She had been obsessed with it ever since she was a child and learned about what she was. After high school she opened her store, selling everything from books to crystals, candles, and potions. Now she began to pull tea leaves, oils, and crystals from a large green bag.

"I owe you big," Quinn told her, as he was about to leave. He felt a faint wash of nausea but shook it off. The sun was close to rising, and he had to get back home.

"I haven't done anything yet. Just try to rest. I'll take good care of her."

Quinn reached out to brush white cat hairs from Faye's sleeve. "You're a good friend," he said. Then, to cover the awkward moment, "What did you do, rumble a cat on the way over here?"

Faye brushed at the hairs herself, as well as some that clung to her skirt. "Very funny. Gabby brought me some things, and you know you never see her without a cat or two."

Quinn smiled, then leaned down and whispered into Lily's ear. "I love you. Keep fighting." As he kissed her fevered cheek, he heard Lily mutter, "I can't believe Faye did that." Then a moment later, "Faye can't be jealous of me."

"Looks like I'm next," Lily said. She thought for a moment. What would a human ask or dare any of these unique people? She was at a loss. Her eyes landed on the highlander.

"Gareth, truth or dare?"

"Dare!" he said, and took a swig of his beer.

"I...I dare you to prove to me you're immortal."

Gareth laughed. "Anything for a beautiful lady," he said. "Besides, I like to show off."

He reached into his boot, pulled out a dagger and put it over his heart.

Lily held her breath as she watched him sink the blade into his chest.

Gareth gasped, his eyes rolled back, and he fell forward onto the floor.

Lily felt paralysed.

Eric got up, flipped the man over, and took the dagger out of his chest.

"That's going to stain," Dimitri said, as he watched blood pool onto the rug. "What a waste of perfect blood." He sighed.

Lily watched the gash from the blade slowly heal.

Gareth twitched, coughed, and sat up. "Coming back to life always feels funny."

Lily stared at the big man. Aside from the blood smeared on his chest, he looked fine, as if nothing had happened. She let out a sigh.

He smiled. "Takes more than that to actually kill me. God knows, I've tried."

"I don't understand," Lily said.

"When I was a man of twenty, I pissed off someone. Someone powerful," he said, his voice becoming deeper, his eyes in a faraway place. "The long and the short of it is this: he cursed me with being immortal. One would think that being able to live forever would be a good thing. But, to watch the people you love grow old, sick, and die, is torture. Every time you come to care about someone, you know that in time, they will be taken from you. One good thing about being friends with vampires is that they stick around longer." He sighed, a wry grin on his face. "But even then, things happen. Hard to kill, but not as hard as I am."

Lily felt Quinn's arms wrap around her.

"Aye lad, you know all too well of what I speak."

Quinn walked quickly down the busy street toward Lily's apartment, wishing he lived closer. He made his home in an old warehouse, which offered him the shelter he needed.

His cowboy boots thudded loudly on the pavement as he walked. Some vampires could be graceful and quiet. Sleek, as if they were the shadows. Dimitri was like that. You never knew when he would make an appearance. Even Quinn sometimes didn't sense his approach. But Quinn was big, loud, and rough around the edges. Sleek didn't suit him. He never managed to perfect that trait.

This evening, agitated, he didn't even try. Lily's words, from the night before, still haunted him.

I can't believe Faye did that. Faye can't be jealous of me.

Quinn thought about that last part. It was no secret that Faye had a crush on him since she was a teenager. Is that why Faye was jealous? Or was it something deeper? He had tried to tell himself that it was just the fever talking. But Lily's words nagged at him until he slept. Even in his dreams, he could hear her mumbled words.

What did Faye do?

Quinn looked up to see Dimitri sitting on the stairs of Lily's building. He was surprised his old friend wasn't wearing his usual suit and coloured tie.

"Slumming it, are we?" Quinn said, and nodded to Dimitri's attire. He wore a tight red t-shirt, black running pants, and sneakers.

"I didn't know what to expect. If she projectile vomits, I don't want a good suit to get hit."

Quinn grunted.

"Come on. Let's get inside. Maybe Faye has her awake," Dimitri said, and stood.

Inside, the scene wasn't the one that Quinn wanted. Lily lay in bed, her hair plastered with sweat.

Faye fussed with the bed sheets around her. "She's been tossing and turning for the last hour or more. Her fever breaks, but then comes back."

Quinn put his hand on Lily and knelt to kiss her. Her skin was hot under his lips. He couldn't read her thoughts when she was unconscious, but he could sense her pain. Now he sensed something new.

Fear.

"How has she been since we left?" Dimitri asked.

"The same, if not worse. She hasn't woken up at all. I tried getting tea into her throughout the day. I've tried different ones, to see if anything would help. Most of it got spilled, but I managed to get some into her. At least she won't be dehydrated."

Faye sorted through the items she'd taken from the green bag earlier and picked up a stone. "I didn't try this one yet. It's an energized crystal," she told Quinn. "They have healing properties."

Faye pulled back the bed sheet. Lily's clothes were damp from sweat, and tangled from restlessness. Faye ran the crystal over Lily's body.

Quinn's eyes blurred, nausea roiling his stomach. "I don't feel so—"

A scream erupted from Lily as her body convulsed.

Pain lanced through Quinn and he landed on the ground, his body pulsing as if electric shocks had shot through him. After what felt like an eternity, the pain stopped. Quinn lay on the floor, panting.

Dimitri fell to his side.

"Lily?" Quinn gasped.

"Whatever that was, it's passed. Are you okay?"

"I think so." He sat up, and slowly got to his feet.

Faye still held onto Lily. She'd turned her on her side during the seizure.

"What the hell was that?" she asked.

Lily's words echoed in his ears. I can't believe Faye did that. Faye can't be jealous of me.

Faye seemed tired and wary. But she was here because he asked her to come. Or was she? "Are you sure you don't know, Faye?"

"What's that supposed to mean? Why would you say that?"

"Because my bond to Lily is gone. You tell me what the hell that crystal was."

"I'm the last one and I have something for you all," Gabby began. "I dare you to let me cast a simple vision spell. It will be the finale of the night." All agreed.

"Close your eyes, and stare into the blackness that is in front of you. Breathe in deeply and relax." Gabby's voice became hypnotic, and Lily felt her whole body ease, starting with her neck and shoulders, working its way down to her toes. She sat comfortably, her mind fogging. She heard the rustle of Gabby's skirt as she walked around them, and felt the witch touch her shoulder as she passed.

"When I tell you to, slowly open your eyes, and look at what lies before you. Do not be scared."

Her voice was soft, soothing.

This isn't too bad. It's okay.

Gabby's voice sounded far away. Lily heard a whisper. "Open your eyes." Lily did so. At first she thought the lights were out. It was pitch dark. She turned her head to the right and saw Quinn staring at the ground.

She followed his gaze. There, Lily saw her gravestone, grass perfectly tended around it. It bore her birth date, but she was unable to tell the date of death. A single tear slid down Quinn's cheek.

She looked around.

Eric stared up at a glowing full moon.

Faye screamed as she ran from men carrying rifles. Hunters.

Dimitri watched, horrified, as flames licked up around his body.

Gareth was surrounded by dozens of clocks spinning in front of him, calendars passing year after year.

These are our worst fears. Quinn fears losing me. He may try to forget, but he knows I will grow old and die.

Lily looked before her. Quinn knelt on the ground, staring up and away from her. The light began to glow above her, and she realized that the sun was rising. “Quinn! Run!” she shouted, but he didn’t move. The golden rays touched his pale skin, and he began to wail, as his flesh disintegrated and flaked away.

Lily stared in horror. When it was over, a pile of dust and ashes lay at her feet. Tears stained her cheeks. She lifted her head to the black abyss. He was gone. She couldn’t feel him.

Gabby stood off to the side, watching them all as they faced their fears.

How can she do this? Why would she? Why am I the only one who’s looking around?

Was it because she was human and the spell affected her differently? Or was it because she had the strength to pull her eyes away? Her eyes locked with Gabby’s.

“Why?” she screamed, but no sound came out. She pushed with all her might for the word to be spoken, to be heard. “Why?”

Gabby just smiled.

“You can’t possibly think I did this to her,” Faye said, eyes wide from shock.

“I don’t want to believe it,” he said, “but I’ve been putting some pieces of this puzzle together.”

“Whoa, Quinn, do you really think Faye would do this to Lily?” Dimitri asked.

"Why not?" he asked, anger coursing through him. It was all starting to make sense. The facts were adding up, and it wasn't pretty.

"That's crazy!" Faye spat.

"Okay, both of you calm down," Dimitri said. "Quinn, you're not thinking straight."

"I won't calm down! After all these years, Quinn, you actually suspect—" Faye turned from him, put her face in her hands and sobbed.

"What makes you think this is Faye's fault?" Dimitri asked.

"She's been jealous of Lily, for starters," Quinn replied.

Faye spun around and stalked towards him, her face wet with tears. "Me? Jealous of her? A human?"

"Don't even try to deny it. I saved your life once. You drank my blood. I don't have the connection with you that I have with Lily, but I sense enough to know that you're jealous and hate her."

Faye glowered at him. "I might not have liked her much at first. But we're friends now. You know that."

"Unless you have alternate motives for being so close to Lily," he countered.

"You know, I think Dimitri's right. Because on a good day, you would never think I would do something so horrible," she told him. She wiped her eyes with her sleeve.

"Quinn," Dimitri said, putting a hand on his shoulder. "Think about this, buddy. Faye's been like your sister for a long time."

Quinn shook him off. "You know as well as I that people can turn on you, no matter how long they have been in your life."

"You asked me to come," Faye said. "And I did. I've been giving her teas all day, rubbing salves on her, making pastes. I've tried every remedy I could think of."

Quinn pointed to the green crystal, on the floor beside Lily's bed. Faye had dropped it during Lily's convulsions. "That didn't feel like a remedy."

Faye bent to retrieve the crystal. She shook it at him. "Gabby gave me this!"

A blood-curdling scream erupted in the room. All three of them turned to Lily, flailing in bed.

Quinn clasped Lily's hand. "Whatever you're doing to her, stop it!"

"Quinn, there has to be another explanation," Dimitri said.

Quinn looked toward Faye, but she had tuned out both of them. She lifted the crystal up and peered at it, frowning.

"What?" Quinn demanded.

She pursed her lips but didn't look up at him. "A seam," she muttered. "A healing crystal shouldn't have a crack running through it." She turned the gem around in her fingers, then suddenly raised her hand over her head and smashed the crystal down onto the floor.

The vampires jumped as shards flew everywhere.

"What the hell?"

She fished a small object out of the debris and examined it.

"What is it?" Dimitri asked.

Faye held out the object. "A feather, I think. Dipped in something...maybe blood."

Dimitri took it from her, examining it. "This is dark magic." He turned to Quinn. "It could be blocking your bond with Lily."

Quinn glared at Faye.

She stared back and said in a low voice, "I do not ever practice black magic. You know that, Quinn. I know things but I'm not a witch like Gabby!"

Lily screamed again.

"If that's what broke the connection, we need to destroy it," Dimitri said.

Quinn whispered in Lily's ear, quieting her.

"No," Faye argued. "We aren't sure what it can do and what risks are involved."

"What's the worst it could do?" Quinn asked.

"It could potentially kill her. Dark magic...It scares me."

"So what do we do?"

"I don't know, but I'm telling you, this wasn't me. The crystal came from Gabby."

Lily wailed again.

Gabby stared at her, a smug look of satisfaction on her face.

"I've had to wait a long time, Lily. But revenge is always sweeter when it comes at the most perfect moment. The final death is too good for Quinn. I wanted to make him suffer, as he has done to me. When I heard that Quinn was in love with a woman, a human one at that, I knew the time had come."

"Revenge for what?"

Gabby sighed, her face softened. "I have been waiting forty long years. I've waited patiently, knowing that at some point Quinn would become close to someone. I had seen it in one of my visions. I just didn't know when. The fact that he fell in love with you made my task much easier. Another supernatural could have a stronger immunity to this spell. A human is weak as a kitten against me."

"You look so young," Lily said, trying to make sense of it.

"I'm a powerful witch. I may not be immortal, but I will live a long time, thanks to my spells. You see, your precious Quinn was not always the upstanding vampire he's made himself out to be. Sure, he's a good guy now, but he hasn't always been like that. There was a time when he fed from whomever he pleased, killing his prey more often than not. Somewhere along the line Quinn grew a conscience.

"Forty years ago, Quinn had quite the party with some vampire friends. For weeks they killed every night. Blood is to vampires what liquor is to humans. The more they drink, the more powerful and invincible they feel. They get drunk on their feasting. During these weeks, he killed my partner, Suzi. He didn't care when the light from her eyes dimmed and vanished. I know because that is when I got there. I was too late. I watched as Quinn raised his head, fangs out and mouth bloody. He vanished before I could do anything. I held Suzi and promised she would get her justice."

Gabby walked to Lily. She raised her hand and lightly brushed her fingers to smooth away the hair from her face.

"Then why not kill me outright?" Lily asked.

"She suffered in her last moments. So shall you. He took my love from me. An eye for an eye."

Lily screamed and lurched towards Gabby. Gabby vanished from her grasp, but her laughter echoed in all directions.

"What the hell was that about?" Quinn asked once Lily had quieted.

"Say that name again, Faye," Dimitri said.

Faye lifted her eyebrows and looked thoughtful.

"Why?" snapped Quinn.

"I have a theory. Humour me."

"Yes, he does, and you'll listen, Quinn. It's the least you can do after accusing me," Faye said. She took a deep breath and said, "Gabby could—"

Lily screamed again, her body flailing.

Quinn enveloped Lily in his arms and whispered to her until she quieted again. "Why on earth would...that name cause this?"

"I don't know, but she's powerful. Ga—She could do this."

"But why?" he asked. "I haven't done anything to her."

"Is there any other powerful witch you or Lily might have pissed off?" Dimitri asked.

"Most witches stay away from vampires," Quinn said in a low voice. "She is the only witch I really know. Why on earth would she do this?"

Faye looked thoughtful. "You know, it could make sense. Gabby told me something once."

"What?" Quinn asked.

"We were talking about past relationships. She said she lost the love of her life to a vampire. She vowed revenge, even if it took forever."

"I didn't know even Gabby until forty years ago," Quinn said, whispering the name, so as not to upset Lily. "We met at a party you held, Dimitri."

Dimitri rubbed his hands over his face. "There were all kinds of vampires there. I had invited a coven, but only Gabby showed up. She approached me beforehand, saying she thought we all needed to get along. I remember you didn't want to go. The party—Fuck."

"What?"

"It was a few months after that big binge we had. After that, you swore you would change your feeding habits. You told me you didn't like how those weeks were a blur and you had little memory of it. You were afraid my party would set you back into a frenzy again."

Quinn remembered, all right. He remembered the weeks of feasting and killing.

"Maybe you killed her partner," Faye said, softly.

"But when I met her at your party she came up to me to introduce herself."

"What better way to plan someone's torture than by getting to know them?" Dimitri said.

"Gabby has a motto, Quinn. An eye for an eye."

Lily screamed.

She had to fight. But losing her bond with Quinn was terrifying and made her doubt what was real and what was illusion. Was he really dead? She couldn't just let this bitch win, and whether Quinn was gone or not, he'd want her to fight. But how?

Quinn's vision of her dying might come true.

Not if I get out of this.

Lily tried screaming, hitting herself, anything that could wake her up from this nightmare.

From the blackness, a deep laugh emerged. "You can't escape me, you pathetic human!" Gabby appeared in front of Lily, looking wild. Her hair bounced around her head as if electricity flowed through it. Her eyes were wide and red. "You will die!"

Lily felt helpless. Gabby had years to plan this. She was smart and callous and hell-bent on revenge. She wouldn't have made any mistakes. Her only hope was the bond with Quinn that no one, not even Gabby, could break. She shut her eyes tightly to block out Gabby's face, so full of anger and hate, and tried to reach him, crying out with her thoughts.

Quinn! Quinn! QUINN!

Quinn felt like a block of ice had settled in his stomach. Could I have been so wrong? "Faye, I—"

"Save it," she said, voice curt.

Dimitri went to his side. "Gabby could pull this shit off, and she has a perfect motive."

Lily mumbled.

"I think she's trying to fight the spell," Faye told them.

"How the hell am I going to find Gabby? Lily's getting worse. She can't stand this much longer."

"She'd have to be close. Like, really close, Quinn."

Quinn thought for a minute. "The townhouse next door is vacant. I know because Lily asked if I might be able to move in there."

"That would be close enough," Faye said.

"You stay here with Lily," Quinn told Faye.

"No way. Lily is beyond our help here. After what you accused me of, I deserve to go. Gabby set me up."

Quinn huffed and turned to leave the house, Dimitri and Faye in tow. Now was not the time to argue.

Outside the autumn air was crisp. The street was quiet. The street lights hummed, and a dog barked off in the distance.

"That's the empty one," Quinn said, pointing to the house on the left.

"Um, what about that one?" Faye asked, indicating the one on the right. A half-dozen cats circled around the house, meowing and rubbing up against it.

"An elderly couple lives there. Why?" Quinn asked.

"I think she's there. Cats love her. Wherever she goes, there are always cats."

Quinn nodded, recalling the cat hairs on Faye's sleeves.

"Let's try there first," Faye urged.

The cats hissed and ran off as they approached.

"What about the people who live here?" Quinn asked. They would be in deep shit if they barged in on innocent people.

"We'll worry about that later," Faye said.

Quinn turned the doorknob and was surprised to hear a small click. It was unlocked. As he slowly opened the door his nostrils flared, catching the scent of dead blood.

Blood covered the kitchen floor. The couple lay in the middle of it, their limbs in unnatural positions.

"Gabby needed to spill blood for a spell so powerful," Faye whispered. "She found them useful to her cause, it seems."

"I hear something down the hall," Dimitri said.

Quinn listened.

"Is that chanting?" Dimitri asked.

"She's probably in a trance, working her magick. As long as she's in it deeply, she shouldn't hear us approach," Faye told them.

Quinn made his way down the hall, his friends following close behind. Quinn peeked around the corner leading into the living room. Gabby sat cross-legged in front of the fireplace.

"We can take her," Dimitri whispered into Quinn's ear. "She's in a whole other world."

Gabby's body convulsed and spasmed as she continued working her spell.

"If we don't do something soon, she's going to kill Lily while we stand here," Faye said.

Before Quinn could react, Dimitri became a blur. He sped across the room toward Gabby. Just as Dimitri reached her, she stood, grabbed him, and tossed him across the room. He hit the wall and landed with a thud.

"Did you really think I didn't know you were here?" Gabby asked. Dirt streaked her face. Her clothes were torn and stained with dried blood.

"Am I the one who killed your partner?" Quinn asked. "Is that why you're hurting her?"

A low rumble sounded as the house began to quake. Next to the fireplace, a large hole broke open in the floor, debris falling away as it cracked open and crumbled in on itself. A hellish orange-red glow lit the room.

"A portal," Faye whispered, her eyes growing bright. She pulled the dark feather from her pocket, hurried to the edge and dropped it into the opening. It disappeared, seemingly sucked away. "There. It can't hurt her anymore."

Gabby sneered. "Hurt her? Hah. She's already dead. She paid for your sins."

Quinn mentally reached out for Lily. Nothing. He couldn't sense her, couldn't hear any thoughts. She was gone.

Quinn had lived many years without loving someone. When Lily came along, everything changed. Now his worst fear had come true—too soon. "I'll kill you for this." He rushed her, fangs out, ready to rip out her throat.

She cackled and jumped out of his way. He almost crashed into Dimitri. Behind him, Faye, in wolf form, growled. She leaped, swiping at Gabby, claws catching against her torso. Gabby screamed and lashed out, her bare hands grabbing at Faye. Faye swiped at her again. This time she connected with Gabby's face.

The witch screamed as chunks of flesh dangled from her cheek.

I'm here, Quinn. I'm okay. Finish the bitch! Lily's voice suddenly rang in Quinn's head. Was she alive after all?

As Faye made to attack again, Quinn stood up and lunged at Gabby as she tried to dodge. Quinn pummelled into her, knocking her down. Dimitri came up beside them, hauled Gabby up, held her arms behind her, and bit into her throat. Gabby screamed as Dimitri tore away another piece of flesh. Blood gushed from the wound. Quinn snarled and attacked, helping to hold Gabby down and tear into her. He heard her screaming but didn't care. Finally, he lifted his head. Gabby's eyes were fading. She gasped for breath. He threw her onto the floor.

"I need to finish her," Quinn said.

"No," Dimitri snarled. "Let her last moments be agonizing. Let her suffer."

"What? Stand here and watch?" Faye asked. She was back in human form, but naked, and covered in blood.

"Look at her. It's not like you'll have to wait long," Dimitri replied.

Quinn felt his knees buckle, and he almost fell to the floor. Lily. Was she really alive, or did he imagine her voice?

I have to go see her.

The portal began to glow. A faint chanting filled the air.

"What's happening?" Dimitri demanded.

They turned and looked at Gabby. One blood-stained hand wrapped around an amulet that hung from her neck. Her eyes rolled back in her head.

Before any of them could react, a demon burst forth from the portal. Ten feet tall, with skin like rock and veins like flames, its wings popped open as it gathered Gabby into its arms. The creature folded its massive wings around the witch in a tight cocoon. Then it disappeared back the way it came. The portal closed.

All was still again.

"What the fuck was that?" Quinn asked, looking to Faye for answers.

She was pale, her eyes wide. "I have no clue. I've never seen or heard of anything like that. Do you think she's dead?"

"I haven't the slightest. But she won't last long if she isn't. We tore her apart. Nobody could survive that," Quinn said, as he turned to leave the house.

Lily gasped and coughed. Her lungs hurt and her mouth was dry. She opened her eyes and tried to focus. She clutched her comforter between her hands.

Is Gabby dead?

She tried to sit up, but it felt like she was crawling out of a fog. A dream, she told herself. It was only a dream. A killing dream, spun by a witch. She lay back down just as she heard the front door open. Fear washed over her, but she knew she was too weak to defend herself.

Quinn! Where are you?

The footsteps hurried.

"I'm here."

Tears welled up and poured down her cheeks. She looked past Quinn. Dimitri and Faye stood behind him. Both were smeared with blood, and Faye was wrapped in a blanket.

"I thought you were dead," Quinn told her as he knelt down and kissed her.

"I guess it took a moment after I tossed the feather for your bond to be reconnected," Faye mused.

"Did you hear me, Quinn? I could feel you. I remember telling you I was okay," Lily said.

He smiled at her. His eyes shimmered with tears as he nodded his head and said, "I heard you."

"Am I still dreaming?" she asked, her voice hoarse.

He smiled. “No, Lily. You’re awake. Awake and alive.”

Switch

Lily put a tray of mini quiches in the oven. She hoped they would be ready when the first of their guests arrived.

"Who's coming to this thing again?" Quinn asked as he entered the kitchen. He tossed a bag of blood on the counter. It landed with a plop.

"Do I wanna know where that came from?" she asked. Sometimes she almost forgot she was dating a vampire.

"Nope, too sinister," he said, and winked at her.

"Eric and his sister are coming," she told him, trying to not think of the bag of blood. Being a lab tech, she worked with blood, but that was different. At work, it wasn't someone's snack. Another bag landed with a sickening plop. "They're bringing Duke and Mary, too."

Lily was looking forward to meeting Mary. Eric, Faye and their cousin Duke were werewolves, while Mary was a regular human like herself. Lily was happy she would have another person to talk to about the supernatural world.

"Dimitri texted me a little while ago. He'll be here," Quinn told her.

"Oh, Dimitri is slumming it with us tonight, is he?" she asked, chuckling. Dimitri was a vampire with a taste for the finer things.

"He'd never admit it, but he likes it when we all get together," Quinn said.

"I think Eric said Faye was bringing a friend, too. She's a mage. She moved here not long ago and doesn't have many friends," Lily said.

"Well it seems we'll have a nice little crowd," Quinn said. "I hope you got extra appetizers."

"I have six boxes of different ones in the freezer to pop in the oven, plus all the food I've made. A werewolf appetite is a hearty one! Especially Eric's."

Lily admired her work. She had two different dips made in the fridge, a cheeseball and crackers, two meat trays, two fruit trays, plus meatballs in the slow cooker and rice on the stove. Quinn took care of the blood for himself and Dimitri. While vamps ate regular food, it was nice to think of your guests' special diet. Quinn had also picked up beer and wine.

"I think we're all set," Quinn said. "You did an awesome job. Everything smells great."

"Thanks! I hope everyone enjoys it. Finish the music playlist?"

"Yup. I will go turn it on now."

"Ok. I'll get changed before our guests start arriving."

Lily scooted into her bedroom. A nice evening in was just what she needed. She quickly changed into a pair of light blue jeans and a pink tank top. As she touched up her hair and added a bit of makeup, she could hear Theory of a Deadman's "Bad Girlfriend" start to play.

When Lily emerged from the bedroom, there was a knock on the door.

"I'll get it!" she called out to Quinn.

She headed to the front door and was greeted by the werewolf pack.

"What smells sooo good?" Eric asked, his nose going into full sniffer mode as he entered the house. Lily heard his stomach growl.

"Lots of good stuff," she told him.

"I hope you prepared for his stomach," Duke said.

"I made enough to feed an army," Lily replied.

"Well that might be enough to feed him," Duke said. The tall red-haired man passed Lily a bag. "Me and Mary picked up a few things. You know, in case he eats everything," he added, giving Lily a wink.

"Hey now, I don't eat that much," Eric protested, feigning being insulted.

Quinn came from down the hallway. "Actually, you do." Quinn clapped his friend's hand, bringing him in for a hug.

"So this is Mary," Duke said, beaming. From what Lily was told, the two had been dating for the last few months.

Lily reached out to hug Mary. "It is so nice to meet you!"

"It's great to meet you, too," Mary said as she hugged Lily back. "I can't exactly tell my friends about...all this," she said, gesturing to the two werewolves and a vampire.

Lily laughed. "Yeah, I know what you mean. We humans gotta stick together," she said. "Come on in, you guys. Where's Faye?"

"Coming in a bit with Emmi," Eric answered, his nose still stuck in the air.

"You guys get comfy in the living room. I'll bring out some snacks. Anyone want a drink?" Lily asked.

Duke and Eric asked for beers. Mary followed Lily into the kitchen to help with the food.

"Is that blood?" Mary asked, spying the red fluid-filled bags.

"Yup," Lily replied as she put the bag Duke gave her on the counter.

"This new world takes getting used to, doesn't it?"

"It does. Luckily we have each other to talk to. The lone humans in the bunch," Lily replied.

"Thank God I'm not in this alone," Mary said with a little laugh.

"I didn't have anyone to talk to until you," Lily said. "I used to have this one friend, and I told her about the night I saved Quinn. That's how we first met. She thought I was crazy."

"Wait. You saved Quinn?" Mary asked, following Lily back to the living room.

"When a vampire is wrapped up in silver chains, he's like a weak, little baby," Eric said, obviously overhearing the question. "Ow! Dude, you didn't have to hit me," he added, rubbing his hand over his short blond hair.

"Ya, I did," Quinn replied, taking a swig of his beer.

Lily passed Eric a beer. "You're lucky that's all he did."

Mary brought out a bowl of chips and dip as the doorbell rang.

"I'll get it this time." Quinn got up from the sofa and headed to the door.

"Oh crap!" Lily exclaimed. "My quiches!" she ran to the kitchen, hoping not all was lost. She breathed a sigh of relief as she took out the tray.

As she put them on a plate, she heard female voices down the hall.

"Thank God, I thought I burned these," Lily told them as she entered the living room with the food.

"I woulda ate 'em," Eric said.

"I know you would have, my little waste disposal," she replied as their latest guests entered the room.

"You guys, this is Emmi," Faye said.

Emmi smiled. "Thanks so much for having me," she said. She was what Lily pictured a mage would look like. Long, flowy skirt. Looking a bit bohemian. Her curly hair seemed to move with a mind of its own.

"Thanks so much for coming," Lily said. "We're happy you could make it."

"What can I get you girls to drink?" Quinn asked. "Beer? Wine? Blood?"

"We'll stick to wine," Faye told him, giving him a wink.

"So, how long have you been practicing magick?" Lily asked Emmi as Quinn went to get two glasses of wine.

"Not that long. My mother and grandmother had the gift. My mother never taught me anything, as she thought it was a curse. My grandmother died when I was four, so she didn't have the chance to teach me."

"That's so sad," Lily said.

Emmi smiled. "Well, I found an old spell book a few years ago in my parents' attic. Apparently, it's been in the family for generations, so I thought maybe I should keep up the family tradition. I started training and learning on my own, about a year and a half ago."

"What brings you to the Cape?" Quinn asked, passing them their drinks.

"There is magic in the ground here, especially in the mountains. I talked to an older witch who lived along the Cabot Trail."

"That's how we met," Faye added. "She found my shop after she moved here. I have been helping her the best I could." Faye loved the occult and owned a shop on the Trail dedicated to it.

The doorbell rang. Lily excused herself and made for the door. Opening it, she was greeted by Dimitri.

"This is for you," Dimitri said formally as he handed her a bottle of her favourite wine.

"Oh, thanks so much." She eyed up his attire. "You are the only one I know who wears a Giorgio Armani suit to a house party," she said as she made room for him to come in.

"Like I would be caught undead wearing jeans and a tee," he replied. "No offence," he added.

Lily rolled her eyes. "None taken. Come on in."

As they walked down into the living room, Dimitri said, "I thought I caught the whiff of dog when I came in."

"What cologne are you wearing, Dimitri? Eau de corpse?" Eric asked.

"Har-de-har-har", Dimitri said, shaking his friend's hand.

The party guests chatted and milled about. Lily made herself busy with bringing food and paper plates out, while Quinn heated two wine glasses of blood for himself and Dimitri.

"You put on quite the spread, Lily," Duke told her as she brought out another tray of food.

"Thanks. I'm impressed with myself. I can feed my guests AND that bottomless pit," she said, as she nodded to Eric, who was eyeing up the meatballs and rice he just put on his plate.

Lily was feeling happy and content as she helped serve people and put more appetizers in the oven. The music played her favourite mix under the rumble of voices from the living room.

"Need any help?" Quinn asked, as he walked up to her and leaned down for a quick kiss.

"No, I'm good, thanks," she said, smiling up at him.

Eric came into the kitchen. His plate was so clean Lily would almost guess he licked it.

"More meatballs?" she asked him.

The werewolf's green eyes lit up. "Yes please," he said, and she nodded for him to help himself.

Lily grabbed a plate and loaded up some food for herself. She followed Quinn into the living room and sat next to him. Everyone seemed to be enjoying themselves. Even Dimitri was smiling.

"So, how is the whole magick thing coming, Emmi?" Eric asked her.

"Pretty good, I think," she said.

"Oh, we have a magick user in our midst, do we?" Dimitri asked, sipping on his glass of blood.

"I'm a mage," Emmi told him. "Well, for just over a year."

"She's been doing great," Faye added. "Come on, show everyone what you've been working on."

Emmi looked flustered. "Nobody wants me to bore them."

"Not boring at all," Lily put in. "I wish I had the ability to use magick."

"Well, okay," Emmi said, sounding more confident.

"Lily, may I borrow this?" Emmi asked as she picked up a blue stone from the coffee table.

"Sure, it's only something I found on the beach."

Everyone watched as Emmi wrapped her hands around the cool blue stone, closing her eyes as she did so. Even Dimitri watched with interest.

Lily slowly opened her hands and little blue butterflies fluttered from Emmi's palm.

Everyone clapped their hands in awe.

The butterflies fluttered around the room before settling back in Emmi's palm. She closed her hands around them, and when she opened them, there sat the blue stone.

"That is so cool!" Lily exclaimed.

"So awesome!" Duke said.

"Thanks. Just some illusion work," Emmi said, and put the stone back on the table.

"Come on, show us something else," Quinn said.

Emmi reached for her bag and took out a pack of matches. She took one from the pack, and struck it on the flint. As the match popped and lit up, Lily watched as Emmi put her fingers over the flame as she plucked it from the match. Emmi 'held' the flame between her thumb and index finger, and transferred it to her palm. The orange ball flickered. Emmi put her other hand over the flame and whispered something. The ball grew. It was now the size of a tennis ball. Lily watched, transfixed, as Emmi played with the ball of flame, moving it from hand to hand, without so much as a flinch.

She put her hands together and a small puff of smoke emerged. The flame was out.

"That is so neat!" Mary exclaimed. "Didn't that hurt you?"

"Not at all. I had complete control. I can feel a bit of warmth, nothing more."

"That is charming," Dimitri drawled. "Can you do anything a bit...bigger?"

"Leave her be," Faye said, sounding annoyed.

"What did I do?" he asked, shrugging.

"Actually, I have something in mind," Emmi said. "Would you like to be part of it?"

"Long as you don't set me on fire, behead me, or put a stake in my heart, sure," he said, and put his bloody wine glass on the table beside him.

"I need another volunteer," Emmi said.

"I'm game!" Eric said.

"Ok, I need you to stand next to each other," Emmi told them.

"Don't give me any of your fleas, Eric," Dimitri said as he stood up.

"Is this something crazy?" Eric asked. "Like, should I be worried here?"

"Oh, not at all. I am just going to change up your wardrobes a bit," she told him.

"Great, I am going to go home smelling like Fido," Dimitri said.

"Ok, just relax," Emmi said, as she closed her eyes.

Lily shifted in her seat. The wine she had earlier was kicking in and she needed to head to the washroom.

Lily got up intending to zip out of the living room so she wouldn't interrupt the show, but she tripped on Faye's foot. She fell forward as Emmi lifted her hands and began to chant something unintelligible. Lily landed on the floor with a thud as a gust of wind blew over her.

A moment later, Lily opened her eyes. She stared up at the ceiling.

I thought I landed face down.

She heard a male grunt close to her.

Did I knock someone over?

She sat up and looked around. She was on the opposite side of the room.

"What happened?"

She gasped and covered her mouth with her hand. Why did her voice sound so deep? Quinn looked over at her like she had grown extra limbs.

"Sorry, the power of the spell knocked you all over," Emmi said. "Let me help you up, Lily." Just as Lily was about to say no thanks, she watched Emmi reach to someone on the floor.

"I don't need your hand."

My voice!

Lily watched her body sit up.

"What the hell?" she heard her voice ask.

"Christ, why do my clothes feel so...cheap?" she heard Eric ask. Eric looked down at himself. "So much for not being caught undead in jeans and a tee. Hey, why does my voice sound different? Why does-"

Eric looked up and noticed her, eyes widening.

"What did you do, mage?" Eric yelled as he jumped to his feet.

"Whoa whoa, calm down," Quinn said, standing up to get between Emmi and Eric.

"I won't calm down! I'm wearing the dog's meatsuit!" Eric yelled.

"What?" Quinn asked.

Emmi gasped.

Eric pointed at Emmi and yelled. "She didn't just change our clothes, Quinn. She switched bodies!"

Quinn looked down at her. "Then Eric is in your body?" he asked.

"Nope," she croaked, and looked down at her hands. Only they weren't her hands anymore. They were Dimitri's large, pale ones.

Laughter broke—her own laughter. Lily's body was cackling. "You're in my body. Now who's the fleabag?"

Lily stood up and made her way to the mirror on the wall.

What she saw was not her own reflection, but indeed Dimitri's. She reached up, touching her cheek. The reflection did the same.

Quinn came up behind her. "Lily?" he asked hesitantly.

"Yup," she responded.

"Oh my God, I am so sorry! This wasn't supposed to happen!" Emmi sobbed, tears welling up in her eyes.

"This is quite the party," Duke said, a wide smile on his face.

"Dudes! I have boobs!" Lily looked over at her body. Eric was making her boobs bounce, smiling as he did so.

"Oh lord, you better not touch those!" Lily shouted.

"You're no fun," Eric said.

"Okay, I think I can fix this!" Emmi seemed to have gotten her emotions under control.

"Maybe you should have your mentor come over and fix this," Dimitri said.

"I-I don't have one," Emmi stuttered. "I've been self-teaching."

Dimitri took in a deep breath but before he could verbally rip into Emmi, Quinn spoke up.

"You're the one who asked her to do something bigger, mister hotshot. You got it."

Dimitri shot Quinn a look of death but said nothing more.

"So what's this idea of yours?" Lily asked.

"Basically a counterspell. Like hitting the undo button on a computer," she told them.

As Emmi dug around into her bag, Lily watched Eric walk over to the mirror.

"Are you trying to look at my ass?" Lily asked.

"No," he replied, sheepishly. "Well, maybe just a little. You have a nice butt."

"She does," Dimitri added.

"Stop looking at Lily's butt. Both of you," Quinn said.

Emmi pulled the coffee table closer to her. Lily watched as Emmi put a clam shell on it and took out a little baggie of dirt. She filled the shell and added a few drops of essential oil. Everyone was quiet as Emmi chanted over the shell.

"Ok, the three of you come here," she said. "And hold out your palms."

Emmi took a small bit of dirt from the shell and put it into their outstretched hands. The pack of matches from earlier was still out. Emmi took the pack, lit a match and threw it into the shell.

"Close your eyes," she said. As Lily did, she heard Emmi chanting again.

After several minutes, Emmi said, "Okay, open your eyes."

"Did it work?" asked Faye.

"I've still got boobs," Eric said.

Dimitri flung the dirt onto the table.

Emmi's eyes filled and tears rolled down her cheeks. Faye put her arm around her. "It will be okay."

"Easy for you to say," Dimitri said and walked over to her. "You aren't the one stuck in your brother's meatsuit!"

Emmi took a deep breath. "I will fix this, I promise!"

"And I'll help," Faye added.

"Can you do it before sunrise? I don't want princess over there scorching my body by accident," the vampire growled.

"My spell book is out in the car. I'll go get it," Emmi said.

"I'll go with you," Faye told her and the two got up and headed to the front door.

Lily rubbed her ears.

"You ok?" Quinn asked.

"The noise. What's making that thudding sound? There's a lot of it," she said.

"That's the sound of every heartbeat in the room," Dimitri told her.

"How can both of you stand this?" she asked, shaking her head as if trying to get the sound out of it.

"We can tune it out," Quinn told her. "Keep it to a dull roar."

They heard the front door open as the girls came back in.

"You find a spell to fix this?" Dimitri asked.

Faye held up an old, thick book. "It's a three-hundred-year-old book, and there isn't an index. And last I checked there isn't a book called *How to Get a Vampire Out of a Werewolf's Body*."

Quinn tried to stifle a laugh but it didn't work.

"Oh shut up. You should be worried about the fleabag in your girlfriend's body."

Lily shook her head. "Enjoying the eyeful?" she asked Eric, who was looking down her top.

"Wha? Oh, sorry," he mumbled. "Quinn's got bigger problems than me," Eric said, looking at Quinn. "His girlfriend is now growing a five o'clock shadow."

Lily put her hand up to her cheek. She could feel the slight bit of stubble growing in. "This is so weird," she muttered.

The skin she touched felt cool. She didn't feel chilly, but she could feel that her body temp was lower than it should be.

"I wish I had some popcorn," Duke said, who was sitting back with his feet on the coffee table, enjoying the show.

"We're going in the kitchen, to look for the spell we need," Faye said.

Dimitri sat on the sofa and crossed his arms.

"These things really dig into ya, don't they?" Eric asked as he tried to shift the bra he was now wearing.

"Least you aren't wearing plaid," Dimitri huffed as he looked down at his overly casual attire.

"I gotta say, Dimitri, you do have great taste in clothing," Lily said. "Never thought I would look good in a suit."

Mary looked at the switched trio. "And here I was thinking that things couldn't get any weirder than hanging with werewolves and vampires."

"You have no idea," Lily said, sitting in the corner chair. "What's that...smell?" she asked, looking around. "It smells oddly tangy yet sweet."

"That's the blood sitting next to you," Quinn said.

Lily looked over at the wine glass. Some blood remained in the bottom. It didn't turn her stomach. Instead, she was tempted to pick it up. Her mouth began to water and suddenly pain hit her as something stabbed her lip.

"Ouch!" Lily exclaimed.

She reached up to touch her lips and felt two fangs.

"Hey, careful with my body!" Dimitri yelled. "I might heal fast, but I want that back in one piece."

Lily noticed the stillness then. The body she inhabited didn't react, aside from the moment of pain from her fangs.

"I...I can't feel a heartbeat," she said.

"And you won't. You're dead as a nit. I forgot what it was like to have a heart beating away at your chest," Dimitri said. "Feels like this thing is gonna explode."

"Hey, it takes a lot to keep that body going," Eric noted.

Lily felt tears well in her eyes.

"Quinn, I don't like this at all," she said, and tears began to run down cool, pale cheeks. She ran over to him and put her arms around him. She felt Quinn wrap his arms around her.

"Oh no, get your hands off him," Dimitri said. "My body in Quinn's arms is not a sight I want to see."

"I feel like I'm about to watch male-on-male vamp porn," Eric added.

"Would you two shut up? Lily didn't exactly expect to be a vampire today. You can't prepare for that shit," Quinn said.

"I gotta pee," Eric said, and stood up.

"Oh no you don't!" Lily said. "Hold it in!"

"Why?"

"It's one thing for you to check out my girlfriend's chest," Quinn started. "But keep your paws off her lady bits."

"Son of a bitch," Eric said with a sigh as he sat back down. "I forgot I'm missing my best feature."

"That's the least of your worries," Dimitri said. "I don't know what's worse. Being Eric or a human."

"There's nothing wrong with being human," Mary said. "Although I am kinda jealous of what some of you can do."

"Oh my God," Eric said, crossing his legs. "Like, I really gotta pee."

"Sorry. I was heading to the washroom when I fell," Lily told him.

Emmi came bursting out of the kitchen.

"We might have a solution!"

"What is it?" Dimitri and Lily asked at the same time.

"I called a friend of mine," Faye began. "We think Emmi mispronounced one of the words in her incantation. So instead of switching clothes, you switched bodies."

"Switching you back will need a different spell. If I did the same one, you would switch again but might not end up in the right body," Emmi explained.

"So what is this solution you mentioned?" Dimitri asked.

"I will need the three of you to stand in a circle, and hold hands," Emmi began. "Then, as I say the incantation, focus on your body, and imagine you are floating back into it."

"Do we say this spell along with you?" Lily asked.

"No, just focus on your body along with these words: body mine, body thine, let my body and soul entwine."

"But I don't have a soul," Dimitri said.

"You don't know that. Besides, you have an essence."

Lily, Dimitri and Eric moved to the middle of the living room. They held hands as they had been instructed.

Emmi took three candles out of her bag.

"What don't you have in there?" Duke asked.

"I never leave home without my bag," she told him.

She put a candle in front of Lily, Eric and Dimitri and with a flick of a wrist they were lit.

"Ok, close your eyes, focus on your body and think of the chant I gave you," Emmi instructed.

Lily did as she was told. She pictured being in her own body. The warmth, the heartbeat in her chest. She began to feel lighter, as if she was floating. *Body mine, body thine, let my body and soul entwine. Body mine, body thine, let my body and soul entwine.* As she inwardly repeated the chant, she heard the faint murmuring of Emmi performing the spell.

She felt a movement of air swirl around her as everything went silent. Lily held her breath. She didn't budge. She was too afraid to move.

Did it work?

"Okay everyone, open your eyes," Emmi said.

Lily slowly opened one eye and looked to her right. There was Eric, looking down at himself. She opened the other eye and-

"Oh yes!" Dimitri shouted. He let go of their hands and began to give himself a pat down.

Lily looked at the mirror hanging on the wall. She smiled. Her reflection did the same.

She was giddy with relief as she ran into Quinn's arms.

"Either I got my girlfriend back or Eric has been dying to kiss me," Quinn said as Lily kissed his cheek.

"In your dreams, bloodsucker," Eric said.

"Oh no!" Lily exclaimed. "I gotta pee!" and she dashed off.

When Lily came out of the washroom, she noticed Emmi and Faye walking towards the front door.

"Hey, where are you two going?" she asked. "There's still lots of food left."

Emmi looked over at her, barely looking her in the eye. "I think it's best I go. I'm sorry about everything, Lily."

"Wait," Eric said, coming up behind Lily. "You should stay."

"After the problem I caused?"

Dimitri crossed the room to stand next to Eric. "You also fixed it. Next time you want to put a vamp in a werewolf body, do it to Quinn, would you?"

Emmi chuckled. "Yeah, sure."

"We've all been through much worse than this," Lily said.

"Okay, I'll stay if Faye is up for it," Emmi said, smiling.

Eric's stomach growled. "Feels like I haven't eaten in ages," he said, and made his way to the kitchen.

"Well," Quinn said, as the room began to buzz with chatter once again. "How did you like being a vampire?"

"I think I will stick to my human form," she told him.

"Want a drink?" Quinn asked as he held up a wine glass, blood pooling at the bottom.

"Oh God, no!"

"Well, it's good to have things back to normal," he said.

"Or as normal as they get around here," she said, as she looked around the room at her not-so-normal friends.

About the Author

Kerry Anne Campbell lives in Cape Breton, in a house full of books, cats, geekery, and loving memories of her husband, Chris. When not exploring the branches of her family tree or thinking about stories (her own and others), she can be found sipping iced coffees, going to geeky conventions, or painting nails for a living. She will definitely finish and publish a novel one of these days, when she learns to stop procrastinating.

Printed in Great Britain
by Amazon

57438365R00096